Hook up To Holidate

PRISCILLA ROSE

Copyright © 2023 by Priscilla Rose.

All rights reserved. Neither this book, nor any parts within it may be reproduced in any form, including information storage and retrieval systems, without written permission from the author, with the exception of brief quotations in a book review.

This is a work of fiction. All of the characters, organizations, companies, and events in this novel are either products of the author's imagination or are used fictitiously.

Editing: A. E. Mann Editing Services

Cover Art: Fallnskye Illustration

Typography: Priscilla Rose

Chapter Headers, Map: Eternal Geekery

Internal Art: Ram (@alta.riff)

Formatting: Jess Wisecup

*For anyone who has ever fantasized about giant lady orcs.
This one's for you.*

content warnings

Generally, this book is very sweet, but there's a few pieces of content I feel like you should be informed of...

Adult language, consensual sex between adults, sex under the magical influence (consent received while not under the influence), vague and brief mention of parental and sibling death, discussions of mental illness and mental health issues including anxiety, depression, and mood swings, as well as difficult relationships with family.

pronunciation guide

Adeib Ali: uh-deeb ah-lee
Alitha Taylor: uh-leeth-uh tay-ler
Augury University: aww-guh-ree university
Aura Nguyen: or-uh win
Barac: buh-rock
Dahlia Torres: dolly-uh tor-rez
Dean Archeron Bariel: dean are-chur-on berry-ell
Elara Lothial: e-lara loth-e-uhl
Freja: fray-uh
Indigo Watson: in-dih-go watt-son
Magia Island: ma (like mad)-g-uh island
Malik Hills: mal-ick hills
Momiji: mo-me-g
Vega Daelor: vay-guh day-lore

glossary

TERMS/PLACES

Augury University: *a university on Magia Island where mages can study and further develop their magic.*

Familiar: *a mage's animal companion, and conduit for their magic.*

Mage: *a being who practices magic.*

The Convergence: *a magical collision of multiple planets (Barac, Earth, Hel, Loria, and Moonflower), resulting in changes to Earth, as well as those prospective planets, including magical beings living on Earth and shifts in our geographical and sociological features.*

MAGIC TYPES

Botanical Crafts: *the ability to communicate with plants.*
Charms: *the ability to move and utilize an object, or alter it, without touching it.*
Creature Crafts: *the ability to communicate with animals.*
Illusions: *the ability to create and project illusions, or images, with your mind which look real to those around you.*
Potions: *the ability to create potions which can change objects, bodies, and other things, sometimes permanently.*
Sight: *the ability to see visions of the possible future, as well as glimpses of the past.*

MAGICAL RACES

Cambion: *half-human, half-demon from the planet Hel.*
Centaur: *half-human, half-horse nymph from the planet Moonflower.*
Elf: *a tall, magical race of beings with pointed ears and longer life spans from the planet Loria.*
Faun: *half-human, half-deer nymph from the planet Moonflower.*
Kraken: *half-human, half-octopus or squid. This magical race comes from the deep depths of Earth and other planet's oceans.*
Merfolk: *half-human, half-fish or fish-like*

creature. This magical race comes from the deep depths of Earth and other planet's oceans.

Orc: *a tall and muscular, magical race of beings with green skin and longer life spans from the planet Barac.*

Satyr: *half-human, half-goat nymph from the planet Moonflower.*

Serpentine: *half-human, half-snake magical race whose origins are unknown.*

Hybrid: *a being descended from multiple magical races.*

Orcling, elfling: *a person born with one human parent and one orc or elven parent.*

Elfborn, orcborn, merborn, etc.: *a person who has some distant ancestry of magical descent.*

Let's Fall in Love for the Night - FINNEAS
girls girls girls - FLETCHER
IDK You Yet - Alexander 23
I'll Call You Mine - girl in red
I Do Adore - Mindy Gledhill
From Eden - Hozier
Love Is an Open Door - Frozen
Glittery - Kacey Musgraves
Symmetrical - Allen Stone
Underneath the Tree - Kelly Clarkson

prologue
INDIGO

"A FEW THOUSAND YEARS AGO, A MASSIVE BLACK HOLE CAUSED multiple galaxies to collide with one another, resulting in The Convergence. Because of this rare cosmic event, many magical races bred with humanity, which created Earth as we know it today. Some beings returned to their home planets, while others stayed. Now, in the year 6004, you can find humans, elves, orcs, serpentine, and many other races, including hybrids of all of the above. With this in mind, the leaders of Earth focused their efforts on advancing magic, rather than technology." I take in a breath, trying not to shake. This is the first class of my first week as an adjunct professor, and I want to do everything right. Augury University is the most prestigious magical college in the Americas, after all. An elfling girl waves at me, smiling wide, and I smile back. My parents were wrong. I'm not too young to be here. "Welcome to The History of Mages 101. I'm Professor Watson, and it's a pleasure to meet all of you."

Although my secret dream was always to work with potions, my mother pressured me into studying charms, just as she did, and so that's what I teach: Charms 101, History 101, and a few other history classes. I blame Eldest Daughter Syndrome. Carrying the load of my family wasn't easy, but neither was the pressure I put on myself either. I graduated high school early and went on to Augury University, where I completed an accelerated Bachelors-to-Masters program in Charms. Unlike my mother's wildest dreams though, I accepted a position here upon graduation. I love being a professor. It's thrilling to watch young mages make new discoveries about themselves and their magic, but I think a small part of her will always be disappointed I didn't follow in her footsteps to the infrastructure sector.

I teach the students an ice breaker. They're to tell me their names, their major, and to show the class a trick. One at a time, each student walks up to the front of the class and does something unique.

A tall elf named Raven, with pitch-black long hair, walks up with a dark, rainbow-feathered bird perched on her shoulder and snaps her fingers. Instantly, the bird transforms into a massive dragon, flying close to the ceiling, smoke coming out of its nose. It's just an illusion, but we all stare in awe at the magnificent creature. She smirks with amusement and snaps again, the bird falling back into place.

We clap as she heads towards her seat, and an adorable faun makes her way to the front. She has tan skin and long brown hair with flowers wrapped around her small horns.

"Hey everyone! I'm Eden, a seer. Professor Watson, would you mind being a part of my demonstration?" she asks, a happy lilt to her voice.

"Not at all," I reply, walking towards her.

"Perfect."

Her fingers are ice cold as she takes my hands in hers and closes her eyes. A few seconds go by, and they fly open, white as snow.

"You are going to spill coffee on yourself in November," she says, her voice now robotic, diluted of all its previous vibrancy. "This is all I am sure of."

What a weird vision. I mean, I know they're never certain, but that's so... odd.

"Thanks for the heads up," I say. "But I won't be avoiding coffee, especially not in November." The class laughs, everyone breaking out into different jokes.

"Pack an extra shirt!" a masculine cambion shouts. He's right, I probably should. Chances are I won't remember by then though.

Eden leans in close to me. "Your future is full of anxiety and uncertainty, but also joy and romance. Be kind to yourself," she whispers.

This exercise was supposed to be a fun little get-to-know-each-other, not an ominous warning from the beyond. Romance, huh? A girl can dream.

one
INDIGO

On my to-do list:

- Finish grading midterms
- Go grocery shopping
- Buy a portable charger

Not on my to-do list:

- The sexy orcling standing in the corner making far too much eye contact

But they say life is what happens between your plans....

"Are you gonna keep staring at her or are you gonna go say something?" Dahlia asks with one eyebrow raised.

I ignore her, trying to push down the overwhelming feeling of desire as my knees go weak, and wave a hand at the bartender. I need some liquid courage. "Could I get a lemon drop shot, please?"

He nods and grabs for the liquor. Dahlia lets out a

small laugh, the pleasant sound resonating in the air. "Make it two, and you can put them on my tab."

Dahlia is my boldest friend and the only non-elfborn human I hangout with. Most folks without magic are jealous or afraid of those of us with it, but Dahlia thinks of it as a fun party trick. It's interesting to her, but not all that we are as beings. She runs a hand through my hair, inspecting it.

"I'm so glad I used that opalescent dye. You look amazing. White with just a touch of that lilac." Dahlia smiles, impressed with herself. She's the island's top hair stylist, with some pretty intense clientele. Magia Island's main attraction is Augury University, but there are some celebrities who live here too. If it weren't for Dahlia, I'd look less like them and more like a wet mop.

"You did a great job. I wish I was in the Potions Department," I say, because it's true. I've always wanted to be a potions mage, but it wasn't in the cards. Dahlia and my coworker Alitha have been working together to experiment on different hair potions, and I'm their favorite test subject.

The bartender places both shots down on the table, and we clink our glasses together before throwing them back. The alcohol only intensifies my heady desire. My blood, like my throat, is on fire at the sight of this woman —at the look in her eyes as I shift in my seat to get another look at her. I turn around and get out my phone. I start typing out a text to Alitha when I feel a warm, towering presence behind me. Dahlia's face is like a deer in headlights, with her deep brown eyes suddenly widening.

"Well." She coughs. "I'm actually meeting someone here tonight. I'll catch you later." Dahlia walks away, her hips swaying in her orange two-piece, long dark hair flowing down nearly to her butt. She's leaving me alone with this woman? Oh boy.

The orcling sits down next to me, a mass of muscle. Her scent is intoxicating, some kind of woodsy cologne with hints of orange blossom. I love being an elfborn, however distant my lineage is, because I can make out the specific scents that cause her to smell so... *alluring*. I have to shut my mouth to stop myself from drooling. What the hell kind of mind-altering substance is in her cologne? Whatever it is, I'm addicted.

She looks at me and raises a hand, her forearms flexing as she places her thumb near her lips and licks it, seductively staring at me while motioning towards my face. "Your mascara is smudged; let me get it."

The cold wet feeling of her thumb rubbing against my skin is oddly appealing. Normally, I would feel icked by a stranger's touch, especially their saliva, but not this stranger. I'd let her do whatever she wants with me. In fact, if I knew this was going to lead to her touching me, I would have fucked up my makeup a lot sooner. The bartender comes by and nods, waiting for our orders.

"Could I get an Irish Coffee? And the lady will have...?" She gestures to me, waiting for my response.

"Oh—uh—I'll have a... sex on the beach." I'm so used to douchebag guys at the bars who order for me that this is refreshing. Still, I wish my favorite drink didn't have such a weird name. It's uncomfortable to say aloud, and I feel my cheeks heat. I don't know if other people experience the same amount of embarrassment that I do, but moments like this make me want to curl up into a ball and die. This is the kinda stuff I need to bring up in therapy.

"I'm Vega, but you can call me V, if you'd like," she says, and I take her in. She's huge. Broad, athletic shoulders lead to swollen biceps. I think she could crush my head in her arms, and maybe I'd let her. She's tall too. We're seated, but I'd bet money she's well over a foot taller than me. V has seductive golden eyes and green skin. Not green like a Christmas tree, but more of a mossy sage. Her black hair is tied back in a bun, with shaven sections on either side of her head. I could look at her for hours, counting every freckle on her body.

"I'm Indie. It's nice to meet you." Indie is the nickname only my family calls me, but I'm not sure I wanna tell her my real name. Most people don't recognize me by look or even name... better to be safe than sorry though. I reach out to shake hands before realizing how weird I'm being and flinch it back.

She chuckles, her voice much deeper than mine, and fucking hell. This woman is so hot, and I am *so* awkward. I don't know how to talk to the people I'm interested in. My latest hook-up last weekend, on Halloween, was with a guy dressed as a Mandalorian from one of the old Star Wars shows. I didn't look much different from my typical day-to-day vibe, donning a black dress as a vintage witch. He didn't wanna talk, and I was totally fine with the helmet staying on.

"You're quite cute," she says. "Tell me about yourself."

This is the part where everything goes sour. I'm going to say I'm a professor at Augury University, and she either won't believe me; or she *will,* and she'll want information on some kind of research we're doing. That, or she'll be totally normal until she finds out who my sister is, and then she'll just use me to try and get to Iris. I don't want this to be about my job or my family; I want this to be about me. Unfortunately, *I* am a nightmare. I realize I'm zoning out when the bartender places our drinks in front of us.

"Or don't. How about this, how about we give each other no specific details? Keep everything vague and just talk as... beings." She takes a sip of her irish coffee, and the smell drowns out her cologne. Bummer. I guess I'll have to get close if I want to smell her again.

"That sounds lovely," I say, feeling as though she read my mind. No specifics. I can do that. "Do you practice magic?"

"A bit. My focus is charms," she says and leans in close. "Though I'm just as good with my hands, no magic necessary." Her breath is hot against my neck, and I squirm in my seat, pressing my thighs together.

I clear my throat. "Me too, although I'm secretly passionate about potions."

She tilts her head, and I notice the gold hoop in her nose. I'd never been into piercings much. Suddenly, I feel much different about the subject. V licks her lips. "Why not do what you're passionate about?"

"Because I'm better at charms, and because—my—it's complicated." I frown, playing with my straw. I don't know what's gotten into me. Normally, I obsess over something unrealistic, anxious over things that'll likely never happen, but this anxiety feels... warranted. I could really fuck this up and lose her interest.

She bumps me with her shoulder, her taut, bare skin brushing against mine for a split second. "It's okay. I think it's cool you do a little of both. What potions do you enjoy making?"

V sounds genuinely interested, and it makes my chest warm. Many people think magic should only be done for work, never recreationally. "I just make potions for fun, so it's nothing life saving. Mostly stuff with food and cosmetics."

"Like what?"

"Perfumes, oils. Right now I'm working on a potion that enhances an individual's pheromones," I say and take another sip of my drink.

"What's your intended goal?" she asks, her voice like honey.

I shrug. "A lot of things. It can help someone sense danger more easily, or—"

"Or attract others," V says as she finishes her drink. She stands up suddenly, the movement unexpected. She walks towards the exit and leans against a wall.

Am I supposed to follow her? Is that what she wants?

I look around for Dahlia and spot her in a corner with an elfling. He's got his thumb resting against her jaw, and I figure I should leave them to it. Assembling all of my courage, I strut up to V, and she grabs my hand, bringing me out of the building. She's intimidatingly tall, at least six foot five. Some small fragment of my instincts is fearful, telling me to run, but every other part of me wants to climb her like a tree.

Before I can even take a breath of the late night air, V pushes me against the outside wall, her lips against my neck. Something lightly pricks at me, her tusks, and I shiver. Her stature is overwhelming—I want to melt into her, for our bodies to form together as one.

"Are you wearing that potion? Are your senses enhanced right now?"

I gulp. "No. I'm not wearing any perfume or oils tonight. Though I have a vial in my purse. I considered using it...."

Her breath hitches, and I embrace our closeness, relaxing my body against hers.

"So you're just that attracted to me? Unbelievable." Vega smirks, so sure of her words.

I'm confused by her sudden cockiness. "What do you mean?"

"I'm an orcling. I can smell you, Indie. I need a taste." Her words strip me down to my bones. She can smell my desire? I must be a flustered shade of pink right now.

She nips at my neck, pushing a hand up the hem of my skirt to cup my ass. We're in public, and I don't even care if someone recognizes me. All I want is her touch. All I need is for her to use her strength against me. She raises her other hand, hailing a cab.

V rubs down my back as we get into the yellow car, easing my nerves. I don't know why I'm nervous. It appears she likes me, but some part of my brain is hyper focused on impressing this woman.

"Where to?" the man asks.

"Tropics Apartment Complex, please," she says as she rests a hand gently on my knee.

I place my head on her shoulder. "I thought we said no specifics," I tease.

She sighs. "There's really no way to get back to my place without you finding out where I live."

I lift my head and smirk. "You could have blindfolded me."

"Very true. We'll have to do that another night."

Another night. My hair raises at the thought. I could get two nights of this feeling? Sold. Sign me up. I'd've been first in line when the bar opened if I knew the night would lead me down this path.

She looks me dead in the eyes. "Now you know where I live, so can I ask one specific thing in return?"

"Of course. That seems fair."

Her mouth forms a grin as she moves in closer. "Have you ever been with anyone?"

"Yes," I say, a little affronted. I've been with a few people, thank you very much. "Less than ten, though. A few human men, an elfling woman, and even a cambion once." Is that embarrassing? Does she expect more? Less?

"Good girl. I was hoping you had some experience. I need you to be able to keep up with my adventurous spirit." One eyebrow shifts up in interest. "Have you ever been with an orc?"

I scrunch my nose. "Nope, never."

She takes the tip of her tongue, gently caressing it up my neck. "Would you like to change that, little rabbit?"

I nod and will my throat to make a sound. "Very much so."

V's apartment is clean and simple, which is exactly what I need. A few of my recent rendezvous were with individuals in grimy-ass apartments. I can't exactly get off in a place that needs more OxyClean than I need an orgasm. As I sift through her bookshelf, I notice the boxes on the floor in the corner.

"Are you moving sometime soon? Or maybe donating some old stuff?" I ask.

She's in the kitchen pouring two glasses of water. "I actually just moved in, so I haven't fully unpacked."

"Where did you move from?"

V crosses this way and hands me a glass. "Now, wouldn't that be a little specific?"

"Oh, sure," I say, remembering our rule. It's fun, though a little constrictive, trying to get to know someone without all the details.

"Far away from here, but still in The Americas. The orc half of my family comes from a few other continents overseas, but I was born here," she shares and takes a sip of water.

I shrug off my black teddy coat, tossing it alongside my purse onto the couch, and head down the hall. "Is this your bedroom?" I ask as I step inside. My heart is thumping nervously. It makes me giddy to see the room of such a majestic woman. It's the small proof I have that she's normal and just like everyone else.

There's a rustling noise coming from the living room, but I'm busy investigating. The comforter is a dark gray, and all the furniture is black and gray to match. I sit down, and V stands in the doorway, leaning.

Her arm touches the top of the door, and her shirt lifts. I can see the v-shaped muscle leading down to her pelvis. I want to lick it.

"Take off your clothes," she commands.

two
INDIGO

I nod and pull off the dark fabric of my crop top. Standing, I slip my skirt down onto the floor. In only my bra and underwear, I stare into her golden eyes. There's a controlling air to her now, one much rougher than the gentle giant she was earlier in the night. V takes off her t-shirt, revealing the sports bra underneath. Her biceps appear swollen, with thick veins sticking out, and it's sexy to watch the muscle flex with her movements. I'm pretty sure her arms are bigger than my head.

She makes a 'tsk tsk' sound at me in disapproval. "Take it *all* off, little rabbit."

As I remove my bra and underwear, I take a quick glance at us in her full body mirror that stands in the corner. We look like predator and prey, her hunky body hovering over me, waiting to pounce.

"You're going to tell me if you don't like something or don't want to do something, okay?"

It's not a question, but I nod in agreement.

"Use your words," she says. At the bar, she was so sweet, letting me pick what I wanted, listening to my scrambled thoughts. Here, she is in control of the night, and I am totally digging it.

"Yes. I will tell you," I say.

"Good. Now, flip onto your stomach and lay flat. I'm going to use that potion of yours." She pulls the small bottle out from a pocket in her cargo pants, and I shift onto my stomach, my head laying to one side against the pillow.

"Did you go through my purse?" I ask.

"Just to get the potion vial," V confesses. "Although, there wasn't anything in there... just some hand sanitizer, which I used, and your credit card, which I did not."

I fight the blush, knowing it's spreading across my face. "Is that weird?" Anxiety be damned, I did not just ask her. What if she *did* think it was weird?

"Not at all. What else could a girl need on a night out?"

I hear the click as V opens the vial and rubs it in her hands. She massages my back, kneading her hands into my bare skin. The feeling is electric. The warmth of her skin, and our pheromones mixing with the enhancement potion... I feel like I'm on cloud nine. She continues down my body, taking extra time to play with the soft skin of my ass.

I moan out, not meaning to, and I can hear her breathing deeply. She rubs my feet, and a relief I didn't know was possible happens. Her strength is undeniable, but I can tell she's holding back, like she's afraid of hurting me. With my height and size, I probably look fragile, but I don't want her to treat me that way.

"V," I say, getting her attention as she flips me over, climbing onto the bed with me.

She's biting her lip while pressing into the small swell of my breasts. "Yes?"

"You don't have to take it easy on me. I can take it." One corner of my mouth ticks up, proud of my openness.

"I don't intend to take it easy on you," she says, pouring more of the potion into her hands before rubbing it into my stomach. "As for how much you can take, we'll see, little rabbit."

She strokes my inner thigh, and there's a beauty in watching her green skin brush against the peachy tone of mine. Using one finger, she slowly circles around the apex of my thighs, purposefully teasing me with every movement. A whimper escapes my lips as I desperately cling onto my sanity, hoping she'll give in to my desires. My craving for her is potent.

With one swift motion, V cups my pussy and then slaps it with a flick of her wrist. Each love tap drives me wild, and I consider begging for more. She presses her lips against mine, her tusk gently nipping at me, and I moan into her mouth as she slowly slips a finger inside me.

The movement is slow at first, just a single digit, though her hands are larger than any I've ever experienced. Gradually, she adds another, and I melt at the pressure falling away as I open for her. I feel feral, the moment heady, and I cry out in pleasure.

"That's a good girl. You're going to come for me, aren't you, baby?" Her voice is low and heated, sex rippling through every soundwave.

V's hands are soft to the touch but strong as they flex and shift, pumping into me. I can feel the wetness between my legs, and V smiles into my mouth.

"I'm sorry," I say, not meaning to drip onto her sheets. I don't want to ruin them.

"Don't you ever apologize. I want you dripping all over my hand, and I want to taste every drop." Her words are soft and full of heat. V kisses me, her tongue swirling with mine, and her hand pressed hard against my jaw, pulling me in deeper. She lets go and shifts off from on top of me before laying flat on her back.

I sit up and notice... she's smiling. It's a wide grin, most of the top of her teeth showing, and she looks ridiculous. The expression is still sexy, but so silly, too.

"What has you grinning like an idiot?" I ask.

"Sit on my face," she instructs me.

My eyes go wide. "What?"

One of her eyebrows shifts up. "It isn't up for debate. Do it now, Indie, or suffer the consequences."

I consider I might want the consequences but move as instructed. I'm a good little rabbit, after all. I widen my legs above her face, and she takes my thighs in her hands, pulling me in closer. Her breath is hot against my skin, and I flush pink.

Lazily, she flicks my clit with her tongue, circling around it before pressing hard against it. It's torture the way she teases me, and before I can muster up my complaints, she devours me, every touch better than the last. V sucks on my most sensitive spot, suctioning it greater than any sex toy I've ever used. Her tongue is powerful, and she pushes it inside me as she uses her nose to rub my clit. The ice cold metal of her septum brushes against my skin, and I shudder.

"V, I'm—" It's too late. I'm coming into her mouth, convulsing as I reach pure ecstasy. I try to jump off, but she holds me down and continues lapping against me.

The pleasure is indescribable, and I squeal at the overstimulation. This woman knows what she's fucking doing.

I lay beside her, our fingers intertwined as she quietly hums a cheerful song and removes her pants. In just boxer briefs, I can see her thighs, which are brawny enough to crush me. I tug at her sports bra, and she removes the tight fabric. Her breasts look soft, but her pecs are still apparent. Pulling me close to her, she moans into my mouth, roughly kissing me, and after a few moments I break away so I can pleasure her. I spoon the side of her body, slipping my hand under the band of her underwear, until I feel short hair. Her arousal is apparent, and I flick her clit. I move so that I'm able to reach her supple chest and suck on her hardened peak as I dip two fingers inside her. Curling them upwards, I stroke her as I continue to kiss her breasts, and her hips buck into me. V seems to lose herself in our movements, and I slip another finger in, pumping my hand inside her.

I ride the high of her grinding on my hand—her using me for her pleasure. It's magical... downright ethereal, the way she makes me feel. I want to kiss her entire body, every freckle and every muscle, every line and curve.

"Make me come," she demands.

"Use me," I whisper.

Riding my hand like a cowboy, she bucks against me, whimpering as I watch her body tighten. She lets out the sexiest groan imaginable as she comes against me, warm wetness surrounding my fingers as I slip from inside of her.

V places a gentle kiss on my forehead and wraps herself around me, my body cradled in her arms. A small formation of stars is tattooed on her left outer-bicep, and I stare at it.

"A constellation?"

"Pleiades; it's a cluster that's a part of the Taurus constellation. My sun and moon signs," she says and gently kisses me. I haven't felt comfort like this in many years. I know I'm only twenty-four, but I spent those important years focused on school and graduating early... I forgot to live a little. The obsessive loops that played in my brain of every mistake I've ever made didn't help either.

"I'm a Pisces sun, Virgo moon. I don't really know much about astrology," I confess.

"That's okay; you don't have to. It's really important to a lot of orcs. Meaningful in the way we develop and communicate with one another."

Her body is so warm and safe, I want to burrow away and live in it forever. My sister Iris, when we were teenagers, wrote this fanfiction about two characters who developed a mating bond. It was a predestined thread-of-fate type of thing, where their magical connection clicked in their brain. I always thought it was ridiculous and teased her way too much for it, but I get it. In some crazed desperation, that's how I feel with this woman. Sex potion aside, she's just different.

The smell of hot coffee reaches my nostrils, and I stir awake. Last night was the best sex of my life, followed by the best sleep of my life, and now I'm ready for a cup of coffee. Stretching, I make my way into the kitchen, which is somehow spotless. Vega sits on a bar stool holding a newspaper, and there's a cup of coffee in front of her.

"Rude. Where's my cup?"

She puts down the newspaper, allowing a second cup of coffee and a plate of fruit to be visible. "Bon appétit, or however the French say it. How *did* they say it?" she asks, and I stifle a laugh.

"How should I know?" I sit down next to her, taking a sip. It has the perfect amount of cream and sugar, and I think I might propose.

"With your haircut, I kind of just assumed you were French... or like... a descendant of where France used to be? However the humans say it."

At that, I giggle. "I'm not French! Most of my family originates from a place called Scotland; though after The Convergence, I believe most of it ended up on another planet. I've also got some super distant heritage from the Abya Yalla as well as from... well... the elves."

"You're so cute. My mom was an orc, and my dad's Scandinavian. He's really into Viking Mythology, I know that."

Was. My heart drops at that particular word. I hope V is okay, but I don't want to pry. I take a bite of strawberry and offer the rest to her. She eats it, seductively ensuring my fingers enter her mouth.

"That's interesting. My mom made my sister and I celebrate all the elven holidays, so we never learned much about Scotland or any of our other ancestry, really. Kind of a bummer, but maybe one day I'll go off-planet and visit."

V puts her newspaper down again. "I don't know what you do for a living, but if you dream of going off-planet, you're too rich for me."

I'm cackling as I grab her pencil, answering the last word on her crossword puzzle. Irrepressible. "Don't worry, I'm not. Just a fever dream."

She stands and turns my chair around. My legs wrap around her, and she scoops me up, carrying me towards the couch. "I'll show you a fever dream."

three
INDIGO

"Why haven't you replied?!" Alitha asks, her tight black curls bouncing closely to her head. Long brown ears point up to the sky, the main physical indicator she's an elfling. Sometimes I long to be more elf. I'm barely five feet tall, and my features are painfully human. Not that it's a bad thing, but I rarely *feel* human. I'm always surrounded by so much magic. It's the most important part of who I am.

"It's been over a week. What could I say now? It'll just be weird," I pout, wanting to slam my head into the table. I wouldn't do that, as there's a waffle on my plate I intend on eating, but I'm sure thinking about it.

"You could tell her the truth, that you have an anxiety disorder and you've been freaking out over how to reply, but you've finally put on a brave face and want to see her again?" Alitha suggests.

"Or," Dahlia chimes in. "You could tell her it was the best sex of your life and that you haven't been able to walk or think all week, and you've finally healed and wish to meet up again?"

"You're both nuts."

Alitha sighs. "The logical thing to do would be to tell her the truth. Or, tell her nothing and let it go."

"Don't let it go. You rarely connect with anyone, Indigo," Dahlia says. "You *have* to see her again."

I pick at my food and take a sip of orange juice, trying to calm my nerves. "I rarely connect with anyone because nobody wants to connect with me. They all just wanna use me to meet Iris."

Alitha puts her long, slender hand over mine. "Iris is great, I get it. I mean, I'm in the Potions Department. We all worship your sister's work—"

"Not helping."

Alitha sighs. "But you're great too. This orcling would be lucky to get a second date with you. I mean it." She's kind. Both my friends are, really, and I'm lucky to have them. I just wish I had the same luck with love.

I pull out my phone, staring at her contact. It just says 'V.'

"Reply. Do it, do it, do it!" Dahlia smiles at me.

I type away....

> **Indigo**
> V, I'm so sorry for taking forever to reply, it's been a week. I've had to pick up a lot of extra tasks at my job this week. I'd like to see you again soon... with specifics, maybe? Just let me know.

Sent. I look up at my friends. "Bleh. What if she never replies and just ghosts me like I did her?"

"Then you'll know where you stand," Alitha says with grace, per the usual. A woman of few words, I feel like she wastes all of hers on me and my antics.

Ping. My text tone went off.

"Somebody pinch me," I say, afraid to open it.

"Check your phone, or I will literally murder you, Indigo," Dahlia says as Alitha laughs.

I open the text.

> **Vega**
> hey indie, please don't apologize. life is what happens between your plans. i want to see you again soon too. i start a new job this week and it'll likely be hectic. rain check for a date? it'll have to be a few weeks, but if you are willing to wait i'll make it worth your while.

Hell on earth.

"Hand me your phone," Dahlia says as she grabs for it. "Please don't apologize," she starts in a deep, masculine voice. "Life is what—"

I snatch the phone out of her hands. "Give me that! Don't read my messages."

"Okay, but what did she say?" Alitha asks. She turns, and we realize our server has been standing there, listening to our conversation. He's young, maybe sixteen, and has been adorably polite... why is he acting weird all of a sudden?

"Eavesdropping?" Dahlia asks, her voice coy.

He shakes his head nervously. "No ma'am, I just—are you all enjoying your meal?"

"Yes, we are. Thank you," Dahlia replies.

He pushes the brown strands of hair behind his ears. "Excuse me, are you Iris Watson?" He stares, big blue eyes staring down at me with excitement. "I didn't know you dyed your hair."

"I'm not," I say, already over this conversation. "I'm her sister, Indigo."

"Oh, I'm sorry. I thought you were—anyway, would you tell her she's amazing? I mean, really, my dad's cancer stayed in remission after using her treatment." The server is beaming with joy, and I can't bring myself to crush his spirit.

"I'll tell her a server at Sunshine & Fries said she changed his dad's life!" I say, though I most definitely won't. Iris and I don't speak these days. We didn't have a falling out. She's just too famous for little, old me, and I don't want to appear desperate. I went away to college early and stopped reaching out—it would be weird for me to contact her now. I don't want her fortune, and I am happy for her success... she's really helping people—

"Indigo?" Alitha asks, breaking me from my train of thoughts.

"Sorry, I was spacing out again." I shrug. "I'll reply to V."

My fingers shake as I type out the message.

> **Indigo**
> I'll bring an umbrella for that rain check!
> Feel free to text me in the meantime ;)

Alitha quietly listens while Dahlia shit talks her ex. Meanwhile, I am just sitting here, text messages open to my chat with V, waiting for her reply. I might not be desperate enough to bother my younger sister, but I am desperate for this woman. Geeze. What's gotten into me? Lust. Pure, unadulterated lust. But there's something more here... she saw me, not my title or connections, and that was enough. Rarely does anyone ever see just *me*. It's always Professor Watson, or Iris Watson's sister, or the bite-sized elfborn... I'm never just Indigo. V and I spent a weekend where all I had to be was me, and I think she actually liked me for who I am. I don't know if this will go anywhere, but I have to try, right?

Ping. A new text from V. I stare at the screen.

> **Vega**
> will do! i'm starting a new job this week, like i told you, and i'm essentially the... manager. any advice on getting my subordinates to like me? i can be quite intimidating, but i want to make a good impression.

I contemplate this. What would get some employees not to fear their new orcling boss? Oooooh! I type away.

> **Indigo**
> Are you good at cooking? Or baking? Bake them a treat or something that'll show off your soft side.

> **Vega**
> you're so good at this, indie. i'll bake some cupcakes. ty!

The server places my check in front of me, and I look up at Dahlia and Alitha, who appear simultaneously annoyed and amused.

"You missed my entire story, didn't you?" Dahlia asks as I place my card onto the receipt.

I scratch the back of my neck. "I'm so sorry. I'm being an ass."

Dahlia waves her hand in the air. "Don't be sorry, but quit acting like you're in love. What if this woman is like a serial killer? Or what if her job is for some company that scams little, old ladies out of their money?"

Alitha crosses her arms on her chest, clearly done with our shenanigans. "I don't think Indigo's new girl is secretly a bad person, but only time will tell. In the meantime, I think it's healthy to keep daydreaming about your future together."

"Thank you, o' voice of reason. I feel like you two are the devil and angel sitting on my shoulder," I say.

"Who told you?" Dahlia laughs.

I get out of my 5999 Toyota Prius, my familiar, Momiji, tucked into the crook of my arm, and head toward my office. Mondays are my least favorite day of the week, because every Monday is the same, at least ten emails from students over the weekend who want my help with something. I love teaching and am so honored to have this position at such a young age, but some of their questions are easily answered if they'd just search for it online.

Augury University differs from every other college in The Americas. Not only is it a magical university, but they built it to coexist with nature. The buildings, made of wood and glass, sit in clusters that are connected by wooden platforms. It almost looks like a village in the trees, but each building is a classroom or office. The electricity runs on solar power, though many of our resources come from employees' individual power.

When I enter my office this morning, something different awaits me. There's a cupcake on my desk.

I set Momiji down, and the white sugar rabbit flops onto his bed, lazily ready to nap the morning away. Though he's very active at dusk and dawn and is a great conduit for my magic, he's practically useless as a companion sometimes. Still, I'm glad we bonded when I matured and that he gets to be my buddy for life.

Moving to investigate the cupcake, I realize the frosting is bright green with little sparkly sprinkles on top. It looks delightful, though it's too early for this to be a Christmas gift. I pull out my phone and call Alitha.

"Hey," she picks up.

"Hey, did you leave a cupcake in my office?" I ask.

"No?"

Who else could it have been? I'm not super close with any of my other coworkers, and our boss was recently fired for inappropriate behavior. *Oh.*

"Could it have been the new Department Chair of Charms?"

She clicks her tongue. "That's probably it! Why don't you stop by and say hi?"

"That's a good idea. Thanks, love ya."

"Love you!"

She hangs up, and I open my door, heading out of the shared office building and out onto a wooden platform that leads to the Department Chair's building. I was expecting to meet my new boss today, though not first thing this morning. All I know about them is that their name is Professor Daelor, they're twenty-eight years old, and they just moved here from another smaller magical university.

Thanks to The Convergence reversing global warming, even though we're on an island right outside Florida, it's actually chilly here in November. Donning a black jean jacket, I knock on the door, now adorned with a plaque that reads "V. DAELOR Mgd."

The door swings open, and I drop my cupcake. It hits the wooden floorboards, splattering on the ground. I feel like my eyes are deceiving me, but right in front of me is V, the woman I spent one of the best weekends of my life with. And now she's my boss, and I ruined her cupcake, and oh, fuck my life.

"Oh, I'm so sorry... I didn't mean to make a mess in your new office," I say, frantically trying to wrap my head around the fact that Vega, the orcling I'm interested in dating, is Professor Daelor.

"It's okay, let me help with that." She squats down, taking a wet wipe from off her desk and cleans the floor. I throw the cupcake into the trash, guilt festering in my chest. I didn't mean to ruin the cupcake... and I definitely didn't mean to screw my boss.

"I was just coming by to introduce myself. I'm Indigo Watson, a first year adjunct in your department. I also teach one history course. Please, let me know if there's anything I can do to help." If I close my eyes and pretend my new boss has never seen me naked, it'll be true, right?

V reaches around me and shuts the door. Our bodies are now uncomfortably close to one another, and I'm unsure how I should react. What am I supposed to do when everything that comes to mind is inappropriate?

"You don't need to pretend we've never met before, Indigo," she says. Her voice is soft, like she's been wounded.

I back against the door, creating space between us, and she crosses over toward her desk. Her familiar, a hummingmouse, is sitting on a perch in its cage, watching us speak.

"I'm sor—"

"Please, stop apologizing. We didn't know."

My lips form a thin line. "But now we do."

"Do you know the university's policies on fraternization? Obviously, student-teacher relationships are forbidden, but what about cohorts?"

I frown. "We are not cohorts. Our employment contracts state that romantic relationships between employees in which one has direct or indirect authority over the other are strictly prohibited."

Vega lets out a low chuckle. "Did you memorize your employment contract?"

"More or less," I admit.

"And I am assuming you are not someone who breaks many rules?"

My heart is racing in my chest. "No, I prefer not to."

V moves around the room, searching her boxes for something, before pulling out a small paper plate. She opens the mini-fridge and takes out another bright green cupcake, handing it to me. "Here. Then at least we can be friends? I still enjoy your company, even if only platonically."

"That would be nice," I say, though I don't believe my own words. Can I handle being her friend? I have enough anxiety as it is. I'm going to be thinking of every little thing that could go wrong. What if I accidentally flirt? What if she flirts with me and I can't handle it? What will people think if I turn bright red during a meeting? The unfortunate possibilities of this friendship are endless.

I sit on my porch, Dahlia on the chair beside me, and sip my warm tea. The taste of orange blossoms sits on my tongue, gently reminding me of V.

"How did Alitha react?" Dahlia asks, taking a handful of popcorn from out of the bowl.

"She swore she wouldn't tell anyone and recommended that we discontinue contacting one another outside of employment."

She smiles with her mouth full and waves a finger. "You're not going to do that though, are you?"

I put down my tea, curling my legs up to my chest. "We have decided to remain friends, as that is not against university policy."

"You told me she has magical fingers, and you think you two can remain friends?"

I laugh. "I mean, she does literally have magical fingers... she's an orcling!"

"You're an elfborn human! But that is *not* what you meant by that and you know it. Don't bullshit me, Watson."

"Alright, Torres. It's going to be hard, but I think it'll be worth it. I really like her."

She frowns. "I'm just worried you like her too much, and you're going to get your feelings hurt. Have you texted your therapist?"

"No."

"Not to sound like Alitha, but text your fucking therapist."

I sigh, knowing she's right. Simone will probably just tell me to stay away from V since it could risk my career, but I can't explain it. I've never felt safer than how I felt in her arms on Saturday morning. She's so comforting and kind... I want to be her friend, even if it costs me my sanity.

four
INDIGO

Augury University can best be described as a series of massive jungle tree houses. There's six tall camphor trees which form a wide-spaced courtyard in the center. Each one houses a different magical discipline and their respective classrooms and laboratories. Charms, potions, illusions, sight, naturalism, including both creature crafts and botanical crafts, and lastly the histories. As an adjunct, I teach an intro level history course, as well as a few lower-level charms courses. Luckily, those trees are right next to one another, which leaves my travel light. There is also a bent tree of some species I'm unfamiliar with where the school library is kept.

Kapok trees surround the camphors, reaching up to the skies, giving cover to the university below. As I walk through the courtyard to the Histories Tree, a charms assistant helps me onto the lift. There are wooden stairs and ladders for those who want the exercise, but for anyone disabled, elderly, or just not wanting the massive trek, the school employs charms mages to run a lift system, similar to major cities' elevators.

Making my way inside the kapok, the bright morning sun high in the sky, I head down a platform until I cross the threshold into the conference room. Many professors have already taken their seats. Adeib Ali, a serpentine who heads our Botany Department, sits at the end of the table where we don't have chairs. His tail slithers around Aura Nguyen's wheelchair, and she smiles brightly at me as I sit next to Alitha. Aura is a cambion about ten years older than me, with bright red skin and leather-like wings. She uses a wheelchair from time to time, though when she's feeling up to it, she'll fly around campus bossing us all around. Aura is the Chair of the Sight Department and is friends with Alitha. One day, I'd like to consider her a friend too, but I'm scared of Adeib. Nothing seems to impress him or bring him joy. The people-pleaser in my heart cannot handle that.

Anxiety tells me that Aura's going to hate me, but I assure myself that, logically, she's warming up to me or she wouldn't have smiled. Adeib, on the other hand, doesn't smile at anyone. Nobody knows how old he is, besides Dean Archeron Bariel, and nobody asks either. Rumor has it he's older than The Convergence, but that's just speculation.

On the opposite side of Alitha and I, most of everyone else sits in a row, minus a few missing merfolk. I don't know everyone's names yet, but I'm slowly figuring it out. My other boss, Dr. Elara Lothiel, the four-hundred-plus-year-old Histories Chair, waves at me excitedly. I want to be her when I grow up. Elfborn and elflings don't live as long as full-blooded elves, nobody really does, but a girl can dream.

"Hey, any word on what this meeting is about?" I ask, quietly adjusting my pencil skirt.

"Aura told me it was legislation updates, but who knows? I wonder if they'll introduce any of the new staff members," Alitha answers. She had her hair done over the weekend, micro box braids which fall down her thin frame, reaching the middle of her back. She wears a red long-sleeve jumpsuit that compliments her long, lean frame and deep brown skin.

There are three empty chairs left. One for the dean and the other two I'm unsure of, but as I notice green skin coming through the door, an uneasy feeling washes over me.

V walks in with Malik, the other charms professor. He's a human elfborn like me; though unlike me, he's actually tall. He sits down a few seats away from me, leaving the seat next to me as Vega's only option. Shit. I mean, last we spoke I agreed to be her friend, but I didn't plan on sitting next to her at meetings. Alitha has a shit-eating grin on her face, a rare sight for her, and I tap her lightly under the table.

"Now ladies, invite me the next time you wanna play footsies?" Malik jests as he crosses one leg over the other, turning towards Dean Bariel, who is standing in front of a projector. Alitha probably wants to perish at that interaction, and frankly, I do too. V doesn't react, which irks me. I know I'm not supposed to, but I want her attention.

I didn't see the dean enter the room, so he likely entered in his barn owl form. Some beings on Earth, regardless of their magical race, developed shifting abilities after The Convergence, and passed it down to their descendants. It's rare, but the dean is one of the few. So, technically, one could say the school is run by a bird.

"Before we get started, I want to introduce the newest member of our little family, Dr. Vega Daelor," Dean Bariel says, a small grin across his face. The dean is pale, with long white hair and a thin frame. His ears are long, and he's built a lot like Alitha, but with more angular features. He's fiercer and much older.

V stands up, and I have to stop myself from shaking. It's not like she's going to get up in front of all our coworkers and yell, "I've screwed Professor Watson, by the way!' But something about this moment leaves me teetering on the edge. She's wearing a deep green suit jacket that compliments her skin, and her hair is slicked back in a low bun. She moves with grace, gradually making her way to the front. "Hello, I am Dr. Daelor, the new Head of Charms. I previously taught at Freehold Magic University, in the mid-north of The Americas."

Everyone claps and cheers, the room bustling with excitement, but there's fear too. Orcs and orclings are strong, and sometimes they underestimate that strength; but it's nothing to fear. I'm probably the smallest person in this room, the elves and orcs towering over me, and I'm not afraid.

She moves to sit back next to me and winks. It's quick, and I don't think anyone else caught it. But Alitha does, and she flicks the side of my arm.

"Now, the reason you're all here," Dean Bariel starts. "The Council of Continents had a meeting, and there have been some legislative updates in regards to schools and time off. We have new rules we must follow about parental leave, cultural and religious holidays, and sick leave."

The Council of Continents is our new global government structure, which randomly selects individuals of specific backgrounds to serve for a limited term. From each continent, they pull a few different types of beings:

a person who was born there, a person who is indigenous to the land, and a person from each prominent population of magical race. For certain issues, they also request members of different identities, including disabilities, sexualities, and religions, to volunteer as well. Each continent has an official administrator which handles all the paperwork and clerical tasks, but thanks to this process, we've gotten rid of career politicians internationally. We still have small-scale community leadership, decided upon by each community, and they're all different. Magia Island, for example, has a mayor. I know Alitha and my mother both dream of getting their names called to join the council for a session, but the thought of that level of responsibility makes me physically ill.

Dean Bariel continues droning on about new renovation projects, before getting back to the important stuff, and I'm zoning out, preoccupied by thoughts of the woman sitting next to me, about how her skin feels against mine. The way her mouth tastes.

"As professors, we must be understanding of students of different races and cultures, and how, for example, one elf might celebrate a different set of holidays than another," Dean Bariel says, interrupting my thoughts.

To me, this feels like the bare minimum. It shouldn't even have to be said. If a student needs to miss class to celebrate their heart out, so be it. But I suppose for old-timers like Dr. Lothiel, this might be a much-needed update. I can recall attending Augury University myself, and Dr. Lothiel being surprised I celebrated elven holidays as she did. I idolized her, I still kind of do, but it left a sour taste in my mouth. The world was complicated before The Convergence, but it's even more complicated now, and that's what makes it so beautiful. I love working with serpentine, cambions, and... orcs.

Dean Bariel moves on to discussing professor etiquette and dress codes, specifically about how distracting inappropriately dressed professors can be. In the year six-thousand-and-four, you'd think we'd be over this nonsense, but no. My eyes drift shut, my body tired from a night of restless sleep. I couldn't stop thinking about Vega and how badly I want her. How much I crave her. This is ridiculous, right? Surely I can't be losing sleep to sex dreams over my boss?

Something bumps my shoulder, and I realize it's V. She scooted her chair closer to mine.

"Wake up, rabbit," she whispers, and I see something flash in her eyes, almost like hunger, before they shift back to normal. "I know he's boring, but we've gotta get you and Malik to associate professor positions."

Me and Malik. If it were just me, I would think it's because she likes me, but maybe Vega is just a good person—a good boss. I can't mess this up. I have someone who actually cares about their subordinates, and here I go screwing up everything because of one fun weekend of fucking.

Alitha gives us a look with her ocean blue eyes and then focuses back on Dean Bariel's speech. If anyone in this world is more of a goodie-two-shoes than I, it's Alitha. She's just always been a perfectionist, and I admire her whole-heartedly.

As much as I feel like I'm going to scream if I have to keep listening to Dean Bariel, I have to hand it to him. He could probably win a world record for longest speech ever. I glance around the room. Aura is watching him intently, an irritated look on her face. Feather McNab is taking notes, seated next to Adeib, who is scowling at his phone. I'm just glad I'm not the only one over this meeting.

"Last announcement," the Dean says, and I hear us all take a breath of relief. "Within the next year, we plan on working towards opening a second campus. It will be off the coast of Naiad Island, in a cave system nearby. This way, our merfolk and kraken students and staff can attend university without discomfort or danger."

Well, at least that's something. I know I would remain at our main campus in the Illusionary Jungle, but it would be cool to visit. I can imagine Professor Rios and Dr. Martino would move to the secondary campus, which is closer to their families anyway. Very exciting.

"That is all for now, everybody. Please do your best as we finish up the fall semester." Dean Bariel walks out of the room. Meeting. Fucking. Adjourned.

V and Malik are talking, and Alitha has already snuck out, likely avoiding having to converse with the others. I honestly don't want to discuss the meeting either. If I'm being honest with myself, I wasn't paying attention. I need to get better at adulting... My attention span is great with people I care about, but Dean Bariel talks just to hear the sound of his voice.

Stepping out the door and onto a wooden platform that leads to a breakroom, I take in the fresh, chilled air. In the winter months, these islands can get down to zero degrees Celsius, and in the summer, up to thirty. It doesn't snow naturally here, but zero is cold to me, especially since it's wet-cold. Most of the birds have migrated farther south, closer to the equator, so the jungle is quiet. I can hear every step as I make my way across, dipping my head into the adjacent space.

Nobody is in here, so I start brewing some coffee. Opening a lower cupboard, I root around for the pumpkin syrup I stashed when October hit and can't find it. I climb up onto the counter, hoping someone moved it up here and didn't throw it away. This is one of those moments where I hate being short. My knee touches something hot, and the coffee machine gyrates, sputtering around, creating a mess.

Did I knock something loose? Stepping down, I take the machine in both hands, trying to stop it from moving. It sprays hot coffee water all over my white blouse, burning me in the process. I should've charmed the taller cupboard to open, preventing this entire disaster, but I did not. I, like a two-year-old, climbed onto the counter and likely broke the coffee machine. This moment is going to loop in my brain over and over again for weeks.

Crossing to the staff bathroom, I open the door and unbutton my blouse. Scrubbing the soft fabric with soap and water, I pray to the gods, or who*ever*, this coffee stain comes out. One of the few articles of clothing I own that isn't black and a staple of my work wardrobe, this top was a gift from my mother, and I refuse to let it fall victim to my dumbassery.

I stare into the mirror, fixing the smudge of my purple lipstick, and give myself a once over. My black bra covers what little boobage I have going on, and I decide I feel cute. I am cute. And worthy of love—just not with my boss.

The door swings open, and I realize I neglected to lock it. Golden eyes meet mine, and I see Vega struggling to stay calm. Her muscled pecs are heaving through her shirt, and her eyes are brighter than I've ever seen. There's something in them, like smolders of fire, as she unleashes herself onto me. Shoving me against the wall, the orcling dominates me with her body as she breathes hot air into my neck, lightly nipping my skin with her tusks. It all happens so fast, I haven't even taken in a breath before her lips are on mine.

"Do you think it's okay to stand around like this with the door unlocked?" she says between hungry kisses. "Anyone could have come in here and seen what's mine. What *should* be mine."

Whoa there. She's being a lot more possessive than she was when I said we should just be friends. I turn my head to the side to stop myself from going too far. I know Vega cares about this job just as much as I do, but her instincts don't; I've got to make the hard decision to save us both.

Her arm presses into the wall next to my head, her mass of muscles hovering above me. Orange blossoms and honey fill my nose, drawing me in to her. Why does it have to be this hard? Why couldn't I have the hots for a chiropractor or a mechanic—a situation without so much baggage.

V's nose, with its cute bump at the bridge, touches mine as our lips brush against each other's, and the door swings open once more. Vega backs away, scratching the back of her neck.

It's a satyr. He's an intern here. I've seen him walking around making folks coffee, but I have yet to learn his name. He's precious, closer to my height and size, but he's only nineteen or twenty. He stares at us, wide-eyed and awkward. "Professor Watson, you're—" His face is turning pink. "I'm so sorry—the door wasn't locked."

Shit, that's right. And I don't have a shirt on.

"I spilled coffee on myself. I'm so sorry for the indecency," I say, embarrassed as all hell.

He smiles, looking away. "It's fine, sorry there's two people in here. Dr. Daelor and I will be leaving." He turns around, heading out the door, and coughs at Vega when she fails to do the same. Our eyes remain locked until he grabs her by the arm and pulls V out of the single-use bathroom. I can barely contain my laughter as I put back on my sopping wet shirt. Sweet summer child.

As I walk outside of the building into the cool air, V follows shortly behind me, her footsteps loud as they hit the wooden platform. I fight my body, refusing to shiver, and step onto a bridge that connects to the Charms 101 building. I'm hopeful there's an extra shirt in my office, but I doubt it.

Opening the door, I dip into my office, which is a building in the Charms Tree that has rooms for every charms professor. Vega, as the new chair, has her own office in a separate adjacent building, and for that I am grateful. I can't deal with how badly I want her, or her body heat right now.

Soft fabric lands on top of me, and I pull the dark brown article off, investigating it. A sweater. V stands in the doorway, leaning against it with her forehead creased.

"Borrow my sweater. You're probably freezing. Why didn't you stick your shirt under the dryer?"

I shrug. "I didn't wanna traumatize the intern anymore than we already did."

"I promise you he had no idea what was going on, but I understand. Your concern is both sweet and valid."

It *is* valid. We could lose our jobs. "I'm sorry, but what happened back there was—"

"Inappropriate? Unacceptable?" She grins. "Don't be sorry; you're right. I should be the one apologizing. I lost control. It won't happen again... unless you ask me to."

"Thank you," I say. "It cannot happen again."

Ping. I touch my phone screen to see a text from my mom. Great, just what I needed today—to disappoint not only myself but also my mother.

"Have a good day, Indigo. Let me know if you need anything," Vega says as she walks out my door.

I don't think I will. I need a Xanax after saying no to that ass.

five
VEGA

Indigo Watson will be the fucking death of me. She is the reason for every urge I'm having to fight. Typically, when a fox chases after a bunny, the bunny runs away... this rabbit might as well be seasoning herself, waiting to be devoured. Between the scent I sense coming from the apex of her thighs, to the way she stares at me in meetings like she's stripping me in her mind, I'm going to lose it. What can I do? Yesterday she said she wasn't interested in breaking the rules, and I respect that... so if I cannot get my act together, I'll quit. I'll quit and move out to the sticks somewhere with no cellular service and become a bog mage, never to be seen again.

It *cannot* happen again, I repeat to myself as I splash my face with cold water. Orcs experience mating frenzies. It's a real, scientific phenomenon. It stems from our difficulties getting pregnant, long gestation cycles, and struggles with giving birth. We *have* to want each other a lot, otherwise orcs will cease to exist. But I don't want to give birth, or date men, so why am I feeling this way? I'm only a half-orc... so is this a half-frenzy? Jeez.

Walking back to my office building, a tiny creature stops on my shoulder, and I take a deep breath when I realize it's my familiar, Freja. Familiars are an important part of a mage's journey. Given to us when we mature, they're magical animals that are blessed with the ability to live out the same time as their mage's lifespan, and in return, they give their bodies to be used as conduits for magic. When we use our magic, it wears them out like exercise would. Most familiars don't complain. However, my familiar is a sassy, whiny little shit. Orcs and orclings usually have giant beings as our familiars: winged-bulls, amphibious elephants, dragon whales. Yet, somehow, I got stuck with a hummingmouse? An animal created in The Convergence. She is half-hummingbird, half-mouse. With my genetics, I suppose it's fitting.

Entering the building, I sit at my desk and sort through the tall stack of paperwork I've been procrastinating. Freja jumps down and climbs over to her cage, chirping a happy little song. For me, it's paper after paper after paper. Complaints from students, ideas from staff, many absurd requests, you name it! I didn't realize taking a job in the middle of a semester would come with so much unfinished paperwork. I don't know my predecessor personally, but boy did he suck at the admin side of this. Best to get some if it done before I fall further behind.

Freja squeaks at me, trying to get my attention. I've been at these administrative tasks for a few hours, and I'm sick of it. I look up at her, and I swear she is giving me her best attempt at a reprimand. Her long beak pecks at my chest, a grumpy expression on her face, and it clicks. I keep her snack in the pocket of my sweater, which I gave to Indigo. Well... that might be a problem. Freja gets hangry quickly, so I'll have to go find her something. I look up at the clock. Indigo is teaching a history course right now, and class will be over relatively soon... I could just go ask for the bag?

I'm walking out the door, Freja resting on my shoulder, before I even think of how this might go down. I mean, it'll probably be fine. I just hope I'm not disrespecting her wishes by bothering her. We're friends... and friends help friends... and it's my sweater anyway.

History 101 is held in the History Tree, which is a bit of a walk, but it's beautiful outside. There's greenery all around me, and I breathe in the fresh air. According to my research, Earth was doing pretty horribly prior to The Convergence. Nature was dying, and the air pollution levels were high. Now? It's healthy and full of vegetation. I climb up to the building that currently houses Indigo and her students. I can just listen to the end of her lecture and catch her after everyone else has left. That's the most respectful thing to do.

Placing my ear against the door, I hear muffled noises, and that pretty sing-song voice of hers. "To understand the history of mages, you must understand the history of Earth, but especially The Convergence. We've covered a lot of grounds so far this semester, and I know most of you did well on your midterms; but the real question is... do any of you remember anything from our first few lessons? Remember, finals will be on all modules. Let's test, and potentially refresh, your knowledge."

She really is brilliant. To teach at Augury University is notable enough, but at Indigo's age? It's downright impressive. Indigo is the only person working here that teaches more than one subject. And not only does she teach charms and history, but she could totally cover a potions class as well. When I used that potion of her own creation the weekend we met, it was *highly* effective, my hormones going wild. Even now, I'm not one hundred percent sure the effects have completely worn off. Or maybe they have, and I just wish I had an excuse for my little obsession with my subordinate.

"After The Convergence, the Earth looked geographically different. What changed?" she asks.

I peer through the window, trying not to be seen. The entire class has their eyes directly on Indigo, all wanting to be the first to answer her questions.

A white haired cambion raises their hand. "Land masses split worse than my parents' during the divorce."

Indigo looks as though she's suppressing a giggle.

"Some places squished together. I heard one country even ended up on the orc planet," a faun-girl adds, smiling wide.

A masculine orc rolls his eyes. "The planet's called Barac."

"Sorry!" the faun squeaks.

My mother had books about the crash, written by our ancestors. A country known as Scotland ended up on Barac, the orc planet, and it moved many other places around. For a while, each magical race sort of stayed to themselves, but as time moved on, we all intermingled.

Indigo rests her thumb on her jaw. "When the new magical races practically fell onto Earth, we worked alongside them to rename lands. Can anyone tell me what The Americas used to be called?"

A tall elf with long, pin straight dark hair raises her hand. "North and South America, which is goofy. I'm so glad they changed it back to Turtle Island and Abya Yalla."

"Not that I disagree, because I'm glad they paid homage to the land's indigenous roots, but why do you think North and South America are silly names?" Indigo asks, a smile creeping across her face.

"They needed a tool to even tell what direction they were going," the elf says.

"Hey, full-blooded humans still use those," an elfborn reminds the room. "It's not humanity's fault they don't have an innate sense of direction."

"No, but it's kind of embarrassing," a serpentine jests.

Not that I disagree, but I try not to pick on humans for their lack of magic. They've got other things going for them, like normal human courting, sans mating frenzies. Human births are a lot shorter than orcs, and are statistically safer, so they didn't develop these pesky, amorous instincts like we did.

Indigo coughs, trying to change the subject. She probably takes the human jokes a little personally, since she considers herself one. She is a human, but she is also an elfborn. They are often at odds with one another, even though the two halves create a beautiful whole. "How many continents were there before The Convergence?" she asks the class.

"Professor Watson, that number didn't change. We had seven, and now we have seven, it's just different." The same faun from earlier says with a joyful confidence.

"You're right! Can anyone name them?"

The tall elf girl with long hair jumps out of her seat as if she were avoiding the world's most venomous spider and shouts. "Alkebulan, Arabia, Asia, Europa, Ice Lands, Levant, and The Americas!"

"Good job, Raven. You all really know your stuff." Indigo beams. "Consider this your exit ticket. Enjoy an early dismissal!"

I want to kiss her. I want to kiss her big brain and her small breasts, and I want to kiss them every day, for as long as she will let me. Right now? She is not letting me. Ugh.

I wish she didn't want me. If she didn't want me, this would be easy. I don't do unrequited love, or lust, so I'd simply move on. It's the idea that she desires me so badly while I equally desire her, yet some rule is preventing us from acting upon our natural instincts. On Barac? This would never happen. Someone would call us into a room and say, "We can smell how both of you feel, please mate and be merry."

But this is Earth, and I have to follow the rules, even though human rules feel silly to me. I was born here. I am part human, but I don't *feel* human. They are small and anxious. Correction, Indigo is small and anxious, neither of which I know what feels like. I seek to understand her... the fear that eats her up inside, that causes her to shake, to blush. Can a friend do all that? Is that what she has Professor Taylor for? Does she even need me?

The door to the classroom building swings open, and a small crowd of youthful faces come out, venturing off to their next class. There are cambion, orclings, satyrs, elflings, humans, hybrids, and more, and it's an exciting sight. I may not always feel completely home on Earth, but I do feel at home in this jungle, with these jovial mages who yearn to improve.

Indigo stands at the front with her arms around herself, giving herself a hug. "Hey, I saw you out there watching the class. Is there something you need, or are you just bored and brushing up on your history?" Her violet eyes bounce around the room, and I can tell she's nervous. When she's comfortable, she tends to lean her body to one hip, but when she's anxious, her body shifts the energy back and forth from leg to leg, like she's doing now. It's awkward yet adorable.

"Something like that. Could I have the item that's in the pocket of that sweater?" I ask, and Freja squeaks, her little green body gyrating with excitement.

Indigo's dark, thin eyebrows draw together as she pulls the bag of treats out of the pocket, and Freja goes flying towards her.

"Freja, let her hand those to me," I say, but it is too late. Freja has ripped the bag out of her hand, flown over to the nearest podium, and is chomping away at the cheese crackers.

Indigo lets out a loud, giggling laugh. It warms my cheeks, and I chuckle. "It's been a day, hasn't it?" she asks.

"It sure has," I answer. "Freja." I click my tongue. "Let's get going."

Three days. I haven't spoken to Indigo in three days, and I cannot stop daydreaming about her. I want to put my hands into that white hair of hers and force her to arch her back as I use a toy to fuck her from behind. That, or I want to hold her and let her cry on me. The worst thing is? I can't decide what sounds better. To be her pleasure, or her comfort and protector. In my wildest dreams, I am both, but in reality, I am neither.

I have never experienced emotions like these, nor am I sure I ever will again. I form a box in my mind, shoving those thoughts inside, before locking it and chucking the box straight into my metaphysical ocean.

As I grade charms student's essays, trying to clear my mind of all things Indigo, I am grateful to be here. Turtle Island is a beautiful place, but I am glad to have transferred here from Freehold University. After my mother passed away, alongside my infant baby brother, the place I had learned to love was no longer my home. My father moved back to the Scandinavian region of Europa, and I got stuck picking up the pieces of my life. I spent nearly ten years in a cold, lonely ghost town, and now I am here. This island is a fresh start—a new beginning. I want to find friends, and someone who will love me and won't leave... But for now, I will just find an open bar. Placing the stacks into my 'completed' folder, I wait for Freja to fly onto my shoulder before heading out of the office.

The moon hangs high in the dark gray sky as I make my way towards the parking garage. It's a pavilion covered by solar panels that protects our vehicles from nature. Efficient and effective, I couldn't have designed it better myself.

Heading to my SUV, a purple prius pulls up to me and rolls down its window. Hold on a second, is that Indigo?

"Hey, can we talk?" she asks, voice shaking.

"Yeah?" I offer. I'm trying to hide the grin that wants to form on my face at the sight of her, but it's not working. She makes me feel light and giddy, like I could walk on air.

"Hop in."

I look at her and open the backdoor. I will not fit in the front seat of a prius. Squeezing in, my head brushes against the ceiling.

"Sorry, probably not much leg room for you," she says and pulls into a parking spot.

Not much arm room either, geeze. There's something off about her. She looks too... plain. Her bangs are clipped out of her face, and her hair is pulled into a claw clip. All the clothes I've seen Indigo don are flowy tops and form-fitting bottoms, with lots of black. Right now she's wearing a beige sweatshirt with black leggings, and it's a little odd. There are circles under her eyes, and she's missing her signature dark lipstick.

"It's all good," I respond, looking into her eyes using the rearview mirror. "Are you okay? You're as beautiful as always, but you look... tired."

"Honestly? I'm not doing great this week. That's actually part of the reason I came to find you. That, and I wanted to return your sweater." She points to the brown fabric I'm sitting on.

"Alright, what's up?"

She turns back to face me, her cheeks flushed pink. "I have a proposal of sorts. It's very odd, and I know you'll say no, but I really think it's a great idea."

My brows scrunch together. "What kind of proposal?"

"I would like you to be my holidate," she says. My heart beats a little harder.

"Your what?" I ask. If I were drinking something, I would have spit it out.

"Holidate. My date for the holidays. A temporary arrangement."

I shake my head. This woman wouldn't go on another date with me because of our employment contracts, but now she wants to… temporarily date for the holidays? What the fuck? Alright, Vega, don't look a gift horse in the mouth.

"Hear me out," she starts. "You want me, don't you? That moment we shared in the bathroom showed me you feel exactly like I do."

"I want you," I admit. It rolls off my tongue like the sweetest sin.

"Realistically, we can't be together, but at least this way we can get it out of our systems before spring semester."

Unbelievable. I mean, could that be enough time to convince her it's worth the trouble—that I am worth the trouble? This might be my chance.

"Why? There has to be something else," I say.

She plays with her cuticles repeatedly, not making eye contact with me. "There is."

"Indigo."

"My sister Iris will be home for Gratefulness Week, and I just can't do it alone. I can't travel back to Octopus Island by myself. If you went with me, I could show you off, and it would make me feel safer," she confesses.

Well, now I understand why she didn't think I'd go for it. This is strange. "Am I hearing this right? You want me, your boss, to pretend to be your girlfriend to your family?"

"No. I want you, Vega-who-totally-doesn't-work-at-Augury-University." One of Indigo's eyebrows raises before she continues. "To pretend to be my girlfriend for my family so that I don't have to listen to my parents go on about how perfect and amazing my little sister is and how I'm twenty-four with no international awards or even a partner."

"It is perfectly acceptable for you to have zero awards and zero partners at twenty-four. Frankly, it is acceptable at any age. Why do you let them dull your shine?" I ask, not intending to let the last question slip from my lips. I don't want to be harsh with her, but I'm struggling to understand how someone so brilliant could let such petty things get in the way of her happiness. It is her life, not her parents.

"Are your parents hard on you?" she asks, and suddenly I am at a loss for words. "...or were they?" she corrects.

"No, they were not. My mother was incredibly patient, and my father left the continent when I was barely an adult. They never pressured me to do anything I didn't want to, so no, I don't understand what it's like for you. I will help you, little rabbit," I offer. Selfishly, it's more for me than it is for her, but she doesn't need to know that.

"Really?" Her violet eyes light up like fireworks.

"I have nobody nearby to spend Gratefulness Week with anyway, so this works out in my favor. I'll go on one holidate trip with you, and you'll go on one with me, and then we can stop this madness and go back to being friends."

"It's a deal!" Indigo shouts, raising a hand to shake mine. "We're going to need to leave Mond—" I grab the top of her sweatshirt and ball it with my fist, pulling her into a kiss. Her lips are soft as they melt against mine. I wish I could freeze time. I let go of her top and give my brain a second to reconfigure itself.

"I'll see you Monday, holidate," I say and wink, exiting the car.

What did I just sign myself up for?

six

INDIGO

The phone continuously rings as I try to reach Dahlia on the car ride home. She must be with her new boyfriend. I'm happy for her, but that doesn't help me in this panic. My finger hovers over Alitha's contact. I still haven't decided if I'm going to tell her about this whole holidating thing. Alitha and Dahlia are my best friends, but Alitha is also my coworker; I don't want to make her uncomfortable. We signed employment contracts, and we know the consequences. Alitha would want me to follow through with what I promised the university. She's got strong values, even stronger than I do, and I respect that.

"I guess I can talk to myself out loud." I look over at the car next to me, and there's a blonde lady just staring... Nevermind, I can just keep my thoughts in my brain. That's fine, too.

It drizzles, the gentle rain splashing against my windshield as I drive home. My plum purple bungalow is in the heart of Sunspell City, where most people on the island live. There are a select few who reside in the Illusionary Jungle, but I like the bit of separation this gives me between work and home. My house is a safe space for my own personal brand of clean chaos.

Momiji is in the backseat, a paintbrush in his mouth, as he works on his latest masterpiece. Sugar rabbits are notorious for being lazy, but, for a few hours a day, Momiji is like a kid in a candy store. He flies around rooms, white fluffy wings fluttering through the air, completing as many tasks as possible. It reminds me of when my mom would tell my sister and me that company was coming over and we'd rush to clean our rooms. That's Momiji every night.

Pulling into the driveway, I park, open my door, my familiar following closely, and head into the house, locking my car behind me. There are crystals and magic books lining the shelves, all meticulously placed in color-coded order, just as I like it. I can't remember if I locked my car, so I walk outside and click the button, hoping it'll ease my anxiety. It does, but the relief is only temporary. Logically, I knew I had locked my car… or at least it was more than likely I did, but my brain won't settle down until I make sure it's certain. It's frustrating, but it's probably my brain's way of protecting me.

I walk over to my sofa and flop onto it. Momiji flies to me with a blanket in his mouth, and we cuddle as I turn on the TV. There's a streaming service dedicated to documentaries, and it's my absolute favorite. I wonder what Vega's favorite thing to watch is…

I won't have these thoughts much longer. V is just a temporary distraction from the hard parts of my life, like my family, and once I get her out of my system, I'll be able to let this go. On the bright side, Iris will lose her shit when she sees her. Someone hot who's more interested in me than in her? That'll be a first. I never wanted to play these games with my sister, but I'm not the one who started this.

I wanted to be a potions mage, but our mother pressured me into following in her footsteps instead. Iris knew this, and what did she do? Suddenly became interested in potions. We were just kids, so I forgave her—but she didn't stop there. In high school, I liked an elf named Terranova, so what did Iris do this time? She went out with him. My life has been a series of steps that I've worked hard to climb, only for my younger sister to push me down on her way to the top. And the worst part of it all? I don't think she cares. She's so absorbed in herself, I'm not even sure she realizes how much she's undermined me our entire lives.

The room is dark, and my eyes drift shut to the sound of a man from Europa describing bird migration patterns...

Dahlia stands in the middle of my living room, holding up two different brand-new lingerie sets from my drawer. One is a firetruck red bodysuit and completely crotchless, the other black and lace matching bra and underwear.

"Watson, you've gotta bring one of these," she says, lifting the bodysuit a little higher.

"I'm pretty sure you bought me that one, and I love you, but it is *not* happening." I shake my head, walking back to my carry-on. We're only going to be gone a week, but Dahlia is acting like I'm spending a month in Europa. I'm so proud of every woman, or person, who feels sexually confident... but that isn't me. I like sex. I t*hink* I'm good at it, but talking about it and dressing up for it makes me feel so painfully awkward. Lingerie tips the awkward scale. No, thank you.

"Did you or did you not rent a condo for the two of you to stay in instead of staying with your parents because you, and I quote, 'don't need the folks hearing me get fingerbanged into oblivion,' end of quote," she teases.

I cross my arms. "You cannot get me wine drunk and then use my words against me!"

Dahlia sits on my couch, and Momiji flies over for pets. Traitor.

"Did you tell Alitha that you're gonna fuck your boss again?"

I blow my bangs out of my face. "No, Torres, I did not. I don't know how."

Dahlia shrugs. "If you're really going to end it after the holidays, maybe don't, but if things keep progressing, you're going to have to tell her."

"I know," I say. I'm terrified of disappointing Alitha. And of losing my job. "What if she tells Aura or someone else at Augury and one of them tells the dean?"

"Alitha is a square, as are you, but she's not a chismosa. She hardly talks to anyone anyway. Quit worrying. Barbara from HR isn't going to read Alitha's mind, nor is she going to fly down to hell to tell the devil to wait for your arrival."

Dahlia is right, but I still hate it. I hate lying. I've never lied this much in my life. I'm hiding things from Alitha, I'm essentially having Vega fake her identity for my parents, and worst of all... I think I might be lying to myself. Nope, no thanks. No time to unpack that.

One of Dahlia's thick brows raises as I toss the black lingerie set into my suitcase. "I'm not packing the red bodysuit, but I'll pack these just in case."

"Just in case you accidentally slip and fall and land in her pu—"

"Dahlia Torres, what is wrong with you?!" I shout, and we both cackle. I walk over to the couch and sit beside her.

Dahlia smiles and turns her head, her long high ponytail flipping with the movement. "Elorthiel has my mind in the gutter, doesn't he?"

"Alright. You have *thirty seconds* to gab about how hot you think your new boyfriend is," I say. "Go."

"I mean you've seen him, he's the hottest elfling around," she starts.

"Alitha is definitely hotter than that man," I say.

"Alitha and you are the most beautiful beings alive, but you know I don't do femmes. Anyway, he has an eight pack!"

"Is that even anatomically possible?"

Her forehead creases. "Well, I've seen it, so yes. You're the one who teaches at a fancy university. Shouldn't you know this?"

"I study magic, not abs."

"You say that, but I'm pretty certain you've licked your boss's abs. Back to my original point—he has a tongue piercing... that vibrates."

My mouth drops open. I *have* been wanting to lick V's abs. Wait, did she say what I think she said? "Vibrates?"

"Yeah. Like a vibrator in his mouth. I may or may not have gotten to experience it on Friday."

Oh wow. So that's why she didn't answer the phone. Damn, the things I could do to V with something like that. The things she could do to me. Fucking hell, I need this week.

"I've never seriously considered getting body modifications besides like... basic ear stuff," I confess. "Iris has all sorts of tattoos and piercings, and that made me shy away from them... but Vega has a septum ring, cartilage piercings, *and* a tattoo of stars. I'm starting to get it."

Dahlia rubs my upper arm. "You're so cute."

Dahlia's new man has two full sleeves and a chest panel, so she probably thinks I sound ridiculous right now, but these are big steps for me. I wear a lot of black, and my house is a deep purple—but that's about as dark as it gets. I'm like a dark cupcake. Moody on the outside, sparkly on the inside. I've always wanted tattoos, my younger sister Iris is covered in them, but needles are on the top of my list of things that trigger an anxiety attack. Oh well. Maybe one day! I've always liked when people get their wedding rings tattooed on their bodies like a permanent thread of fate.

Dahlia waves her hands in front of my face, her tan wrist covered in golden bangles. "Earth to Indigo—I've got a client first thing tomorrow morning, so I've gotta head out soon. Are you ready to see your parents?"

"Not in the slightest, but I'm not sure I'll ever be," I say. I moved here for school, stayed for work, but ultimately I think I just didn't want to go back. The island itself has done nothing wrong, but it's home, which means it's also the origins of all my trauma. I should be grateful that my life is good, but sometimes existing is so... hard.

"Try and enjoy being home, but if you don't, just sneak away with your new fuck buddy," Dahlia says with a wink. She pulls me in for a hug, and I accept it. She gets up off the couch, grabs her bag, and heads out my front door.

I rub my hands in my face. What have I got myself into?

Vega and I sit on the ferry, the morning mist rising above the sea, and run through our backstory as if we're two actors rehearsing our lines. V rolls up the brown sleeves of her sweatshirt, and my eyes wander to her exposed skin. Her hands are pressed against the bench, causing the veins in the crook of her elbow to emerge in prominent lines.

"I'm still Vega Daelor, twenty-eight years old, and I'm still from Freehold, a community in the central north-east part of Turtle Island. What can't they know?" she asks. My brain is still running through hundreds of things I wouldn't want them to know that'll never come up, like the way she sounds when I touch her.

"They can't know you work at Augury University," I remind her. Our thighs are close enough to touch, though hers are much larger. Even through the fabric of her dress pants, I can see the prominence of her quads.

"Should I even share that I practice magic?"

"Yes. My mother is an experienced charms mage, who works as an engineer. I want her to be impressed with you and to know you're skilled."

Vega purses her lips. "Is that why you're a charms professor?"

"Huh?"

"You did what would make your mother happy, not what would make you happy."

How did she figure that out? V's golden eyes stare into mine, and it's like she's seeing me. All of me. Her gaze is shattering the glass box I built around my heart, reading me like a book that's begging to be opened. She takes her time, caressing every page, and I feel so vulnerable.

I cough, desperate to change the subject. "So, what job should we say you have? It needs to be something you can discuss in great detail. I'll do my best to make sure they don't pick our story apart."

"The only things I can discuss in great detail are charms, stars, and how badly I want to take your clothes off. You choose." She bites her bottom lip, one eyebrow raising, and I swear my entire body was just set on fire.

"You're into working out. Could we choose something like that?" I say, refusing to give in to my desire.

"Sure. I'll say I design and work on fitness equipment."

"Perfect." I turn away from her, shifting my body and staring out into the sea. The water is crystal clear, and there are small octopi scattered throughout these depths in every color. We must be nearing Octopus Island.

seven

VEGA

Indigo looks like a pile of nervous energy. One of her hands is clasped over the other to hide her shaking, and she's lost her beautiful smile in this anxious daze. I want to wrap my body around hers, skin on skin, but we're in public, so instead I pull her legs over mine and rest a hand on her thigh. It's a little romantic in gesture, but nothing too far. I just need her to know I can anchor her and all the big emotions she's experiencing.

The ferry docks, and we get in line to exit, both of our familiars in tow. Octopus Island is only a few hours from the Northern part of Magia Island, where we departed from. I've never been, but it seems to be a popular destination. There's tons of humans and elves as we get off, even an orc. He stands nearby, and I nod at him in recognition.

The people traveling to Octopus Island all look like they're going home or visiting a loved one, just as Indigo does, and I get the feeling it isn't exactly a tourist destination. Sleeping Island, which is another island in the Magia Archipelago, is. I've heard many great things about their events and celebrations. It's honestly a bit odd how little I've heard about Octopus Island in comparison.

Indigo widens her violet eyes, jolting me from my chain of thoughts.

"I have a lot of baggage," she says, and I look at her with my eyebrows furrowed. The line is moving forward.

"All you brought was that little suitcase," I say, half-teasing. I'm pretty sure that's not what she meant, but I say it anyway to ease the tension. We step off the platform and onto the dock.

Indigo smiles and tilts her head, giving me a funny look. "No, V, I mean emotional baggage. You're going to witness a lot of it this week. I love my family, but you'll see all the bad stuff too." She rubs her hands down her face. "My own anxiety, my mother struggles with her mental health, my father has no backbone, and my sister and I can't seem to fucking get along. *That's* why I never visit home. It's a lot." There's the faint welt of tears in those violet eyes, and my blood boils. If her family manages to make her feel this awful when they aren't around, it's going to be a struggle to hold my tongue when I meet them.

"You made a good choice in bringing me with you. I can carry you through this week, and I'm strong enough for you and all your baggage, no matter how much it weighs you down." We walk towards a line of cars, looking for our rental.

"You think you can handle a week with a walking, talking anxiety disorder with mommy issues?"

"Do you think you can handle a week with a lonely orc who's got a dead mom and daddy issues?" I retort. I'm not afraid of her mind or her pain. I've weathered just as bad of storms myself.

"Jeez, Vega," she says, her bright eyes wide with shock.

A tall, lanky human approaches us with a set of keys. "Indigo Watson?" he inquires, and she nods, pulling out her I.D. He hands her the keys, and she pops open the trunk of the silver SUV. Placing our bags inside, I close the trunk and get into the passenger side.

Indigo is in a knee-length black dress with long sleeves. She presses the start-up button, the car pulling energy from its magi-battery, and I buckle my seatbelt, ready for the week ahead. It's a week of service, a week of convincing her family that their daughter is good enough, when the reality is that she's better. It is also a week to convince her that I am worth the trouble. A week for *my* brain to figure out how we can continue seeing one another without *her* brain falling apart, scared everything will be ripped at the seams. Here's to hoping nobody from work spots us.

I won't let this woman go without a fight. Sometimes it's impossible to even approach women... they see a massive orc approaching them and balk. Afraid of the big bad magical wolf. Orcs are massive, sure, but that doesn't make us dangerous. To be fair, men have a history of being dangerous towards women for thousands of years, and it's only recently gotten better. If I were a small woman without magic, I'd probably be afraid of a big muscled being, man or not, too.

But I've rarely felt a connection like this. I've been so busy picking up the broken pieces of my life that I forgot to find someone I want to use my strength to protect. That is, until now. I sound ridiculous... I'm not in love, we barely know each other, but something tells me Indigo is worth falling for.

Pulling into the complex of the condo we rented for the week, Indigo's face is turning red as she parks in the garage. Momiji and Freja are asleep next to one another in the backseat, and I try my best not to wake them.

"Everything okay?"

"Yeah! Everything's fine." Her voice is chipper. *Too* chipper.

I unbuckle the seatbelt, open the door and get out to stretch. "Pop the trunk, and I'll get our bags," I say.

"You sure? I don't mind grabbing mine."

"I'd be mildly offended if you did," I jest. I wouldn't, she's free to do whatever she likes, but I love doing things for her. I want to do everything for her, she can even make me a honey-do list. I know she loves to-do lists. I spotted one in her office, and if it wasn't at work, I would have added my name straight to the top.

I grab our suitcases and follow her short but delicious legs as they take us to an elevator. Indigo is holding a blanket, carrying both of our sleeping familiars within it, like a magical burrito. It's a little after noon, early for a nap, and I theorize Freja is faking being asleep so that she can be with Momiji. Whatever.

We get inside, and, right before the door closes, a man steps in. He's human with short blonde hair. There isn't even the faintest scent of magic on him. Donning some sort of human sports jersey, beer in hand, he looks like every man your mother warns you about as a child. "Hey sexy," he says, words slurred, in Indigo's direction. "You look like you'd sound as pretty as you look underneath me." What the fuck kind of drunken pickup line is that?

"Huh—no—" she stutters, and I can feel the adrenaline coursing through me, waves of anger racing to reach the surface of my tongue.

I'm pretty certain Indigo would hate me if I went full protective asshole mode on this man, but I don't know what else to do. I have to fight the snarl that wants to escape my lips as he takes one stumbling step closer to her. He takes another, and I flick my wrist, magic spraying out of me, clipping his clothing to the wall. Legally, we're not supposed to use magic to harm others, but I didn't use any on *him*. I simply charmed his clothes to the wall. He struggles, confused at why he can't move, and I laugh.

Indigo looks at me like a sad little rabbit, and I consider hitting him for good measure but decide I've got better things to be doing. We get off the elevator and she pulls out her phone, typing in a code so we can enter the condo. "Is he stuck in the elevator?" she asks, voice quiet as we walk inside. She looks simultaneously relieved and concerned, and I feel bad. My goal was to protect her, not upset her. The prick deserved worse.

"It'll wear off in a few hours," I say, putting the bags down.

Walking through the condo, it's nice. A little more vibrant than either of our styles, but it'll be a great vacation stay. I go searching for the bedrooms, only to find just one. That's odd. Heading back into the kitchen, I spot Indigo, who is leaning against the counter table. "Hey, I'm going to head downstairs and talk to the front desk to get our condo changed," I tell her.

"Wait, why? I got this condo through an app; the front desk can't help us. What's wrong?"

"There's only one bedroom and only one bed."

Her cheeks flush pink almost instantly, and she scratches the back of her head, looking down at the floor. "I picked the condo myself."

"Pardon?"

"I... I—you don't want to do this? I thought—hooboy, this is awkward; I'm so sorry." Her voice is all stutters and slurred words as she apologizes, and she drops her face into her hands.

"Don't apologize; what is there to be sorry for?" I know she's anxious, I get that, but I actually don't know what about this time.

"I asked you to be my 'holidate' and you agreed, which was very kind of you, but I thought you wanted to come along because... well, we were going to get each other out of our systems. Now I'm realizing maybe you don't struggle with the same desires for me as I do for you. I might've misread the whole bathroom lack-of-shirt event." She thinks I don't want her? How? I've been working so hard not to appear desperate for her.

"Do you think I don't want you?" I ask in earnest.

She shrugs. "I mean, separate bedrooms...."

This woman needs a fucking confidence booster, because fucking hell. Who wouldn't want Indie? I strut towards her, and she gasps as I pull her into a kiss. It's deep, and I slide my tongue into her mouth, relishing in her warmth. I break, placing her face in the palm of my hands, and open my eyes.

I stare at her for a moment, our eyes transfixed on one another's, and press our noses together. "I want you. Ever since we met, you've invaded my every thought. I can't get you out of my head, so please tell that part of your brain, the part that says you're not wanted, to kindly fuck off."

She smiles at me. It's small, but I know she believes me. I take one hand, gliding it up her dress, and use the other to grip her hair at the nape of her neck. I pull her head back, baring her throat to me, and suck on it gently. As my left hand reaches the fabric of her underwear, I consider how I should ask to go further.

Ring. Ring.

What is that?

Ring. Ring.

Fuck me. Indigo shifts, and I let go of her as she runs over to the couch to grab her phone, clearly trying not to wake Momiji and Freja, who are still sound asleep. She presses a button, and the phone stops ringing, but she's staring at it for what feels like eternity. Sliding her finger across the screen, she answers it.

"Hello, Mother; how're you?"

There's a long silence, and I can visibly see Indigo's tension grow. She's standing, stiff as a board, her shoulders tight.

"Yes, we can be there for dinner tonight. Yes, I'm glad you're excited to meet her."

There's another long pause.

"Five p.m. We'll be there. See you soon!"

Indigo hangs up the phone, and her body relaxes. She looks at me with big, doe-like eyes.

"Dinner... tonight? I thought we weren't supposed to see them until tomorrow," I say, breaking the silence.

"We weren't, but my mother decided to cook and that means we have to go tonight."

"We don't *have* to."

She shakes her head. "No, we have to."

"Do we have time for a quickie?" I jest. I don't mean it. Though I haven't known Indigo for very long, I feel a connection to her that's borderline cosmic. From what I do know, I'm pretty sure she's shut down, her body giving in to the waves of anxiety that are passing through her.

My guess is confirmed when she just stares at me blankly.

"I was kidding," I say, in hopes it'll pull her out of this catatonic state. She stands there, body immobile. I pick her up, and she's a statue in my arms as I carry her to the bedroom and throw her onto the bed.

"I thought you were kidding," she mumbles, waking out of her fog, but still distressed.

"I need your help picking out what I should wear," I say, grabbing a vest and a jacket out of the suitcase. I hold them both up, and she scrunches her brows.

"What shirt are you going to wear?"

"Uh, a white one?"

"Meh. Go with the jacket then. Black vest and white top kinda give off flight attendant or server vibes, and that'll just make my mom act weird."

I frown. "Is your mother one of those awful people who are rude to service workers?"

"No, but like... she's a snob, so it's better to avoid anything that could cause her to look down on us," she admits, and my skin chills. I'd rather have the ashes and memories of a wonderful mom, than a living breathing monster for one.

Sometimes I forget that *I'm* a monster. I mean, I'm not... at least not in the brutal, evil villain way from old human folklore, but I am in the sense that I am bigger and stronger than humanity could ever hope to be, but I like that about myself. Indigo's safe with me because I can confidently say that I could beat up any man that comes near her, with the exception of an orc, and orcs wouldn't touch her. Not unless my scent was off of her, but that'll take months. Months I won't allow to go by. I want her to reek of me indefinitely.

Putting on the black suit jacket and dress pants, I lift her off the bed, throwing her body over my shoulder. Indigo squirms, fighting to be let down, but it's all a ruse. She's magical. If she wanted to get down, she would, but I think she enjoys the fight. She grabs for my ass, and I think if she could reach, she'd try and take a bite.

"Where are you taking me?" she yelps.

"To your parents house."

eight
VEGA

Indigo's childhood home is painted white with cute, simple decor. It's not *overly* lavish, but it does sort of look like something out of a home decor magazine. We pull up to the driveway, where three luxury cars are already parked. The car we rented is a simple baseline SUV, which I manage to squeeze into the remaining space. Stepping out, I run over to open the door for Indie. I'd open it for her anyway, but I make a show out of it in case her family is watching through the window. I've made it my mission this week to show them that if they won't care for their daughter and make her feel appreciated, someone else will.

We walk up, hand in hand, and she knocks on the door. It's a soft knock, and for a moment I'm not sure they can hear it. The door swings open, but nobody is there.

Did Indigo's mother seriously charm the door open?

"Mom, Dad, I'm here," Indigo says, her voice shaky. She's nervous, and I'd do anything to make the emotion go away for her.

I've only met a few of my ex-girlfriends' parents, but I don't remember feeling nervous. Holidating or for real, what are they gonna do, tell a grown woman no? Besides, I'm great at winning people over.

As we cross through a corridor, I note the pictures on the wall. There's wedding photos of Indigo's parents—Mr. Watson is a tan white man with brown eyes and chestnut brown hair, and Mrs. Watson, a beanpole of a woman, with bright white hair and violet eyes, just like Indie's. They look happy, but stuck up. Almost like they're too good for their own wedding.

There are a few family photos of the four of them, and Indigo's sister mirrors Indigo well, just with darker features. As we continue down the hall, the dynamics change. All of the pictures are of Iris. There's a damn-near shrine to the girl. A screen is mounted to the wall, presenting a slideshow of online articles and social media posts about Iris and her accomplishments. *Shit.* Iris Watson, Indigo's younger sister, invented the potion that stopped cancer cells from recurring. The pieces are all falling into place, and now I get why Indigo is so nervous. Those are impossible shoes to fill. I can't believe I hadn't put two and two together.

Crossing over a lip in the floor, we enter a living room. There's a big sign in cursive that says "it's a good day for a good day," and I decide the only thing worse than that would've been "Live. Laugh. Love." I mean, what the fuck does that even mean? Isn't every day a good day to be... a good... I don't have the mental energy for this ridiculousness. The only saving grace for this room is that there's a corner of beautiful art from different cultures. Scotland, I think is one of them, and Elven culture, as well as a quilted piece of art in bright colors. It's all so unique and lovely, and each part of it represents a fragment of who Indigo is. Who her family is too.

"Your girlfriend must be mesmerized by our house or something," a man whispers from the corner.

I cough. I didn't realize they were all sitting there waiting for my introduction. "Hello, I'm Vega."

"Hi, Vega, nice to meet you," Mr. Watson says, standing up to shake my hand. His grip is firm, but mine is firmer.

Mrs. Watson stands and smiles, but it doesn't meet her eyes. She's wearing gray slacks and a white blouse. If it weren't for her hair and eye color, which are the same as Indigo's, I wouldn't think the woman was of elven descent. She's thin, as most elves are, but she isn't tall, which is rare for an elfborn. She's only a few inches above five feet, and her husband only an inch or two taller than that. I'm not complaining though; I love how much smaller in stature Indigo is to me.

"Why don't we have dinner, now that we're all here," Mrs. Watson says, heading out through another corridor.

Something moves on the couch behind me, and Iris comes out of nowhere. Her body was sinking into the sofa, being absorbed by the many decorative pillows. She looks a lot like Indigo, though she exudes more confidence. Tattoos cover her arms and some of her legs, and her outfit is a lot bolder, a black romper with a low v that exposes her cleavage. She's not what I expected. I try not to look, try not to notice her at all. I thought Indigo's 'perfect' younger sister would look less... punk rock.

"Hey, Indie," Iris says. I try to read Indigo's expression, attempting to guess what she'll say, but I haven't a clue.

"Hey." Her voice is a whisper. "I hope you're doing well. Mom says you won another award."

"Yeah, I'm okay," Iris replies, smiling wide.

We follow the Watsons until we come into a vast dining room. The table is a deep, red mahogany, with legs which spiral down in a decorative pattern. It's classical. To my surprise, the table is empty.

"Please, have a seat," Mr. Watson instructs us.

Mrs. Watson tucks her long, white strands behind her ears, and I can see they come to slight points, unlike her daughters'. "Vega, is it?"

"Yes ma'am," I say.

"Would you be a dear and help set the table?" she asks, and I nod, standing up.

She shakes her head. "No need, just use your magic."

I nod, understanding her meaning. Magic is complicated. Any mage can technically utilize any kind of magic, but it won't come naturally to them. Instinctually, when completing day-to-day tasks, you'll lean towards the magic type you're inclined to. I am truly a charms type, but I don't use my magic for frivolous things. Sex? Sure. An emergency? Absolutely. But setting the table? That feels like a waste of my and Freja's energy. Still... This is a test, and I'm not one to fail.

I flick my wrist, and my magic seeps out. Using my senses, I scent the cupboards which house what we need to set the table. A long table cloth flies out, alongside fine dining wear. The objects dance through the air, and as I neatly set things down, Mrs. Watson uses her own magic to bring in the food from the kitchen. It looks like a scene out of an old classic Disney movie I remember seeing as a child, and Iris and Mr. Watson look in awe of our show. Indigo, on the other hand, is glowering at us, and I fear I've made a mistake in passing this test.

"Excellent. Indigo would always drop something when we attempted that," Mrs. Watson says.

Fuck me. I didn't mean to one-up my girlfriend. *My very temporary holiday girlfriend*, I remind myself.

Mr. Watson pours himself a glass of wine and gulps it down in one sip. He must know something we don't.

Mrs. Watson clears her throat. "It's a wonder the most prestigious magical school in the nation hired her. She was never very good at charms—"

"Mom, that's enough. You know damn well that Indigo was hired because of how good she is at teaching. She might not be the best charms mage, but she's likely creating the best charms mages, some even better than you," Iris interrupts.

My blood boils at the way Indigo is being discussed. I'm glad Iris stood up for her sister, because if she hadn't, I was surely going to get myself in trouble. I knew there was going to be family drama, but I wrongly assumed it would take a few days into the trip. I don't want to make this worse for Indie, but the best way to protect her right now is to get her the fuck out of here.

Indigo looks at me, tears welting in her eyes, and I pull her hand, eyebrows raised. She nods, and I help her rise from her seat. Her hands are shaking as one intertwines with mine. Looking at the table, I go to speak, but nothing comes out. I've never been stunned into silence before; this is a first.

As we make our way out of the snobbish, cold house, I open the silver door of the SUV and help Indigo inside. Kissing her forehead, I lift my hand and wipe away a single tear.

Indigo sits on the balcony of the condo we're staying in, a plush white blanket wrapped around her body. My heart aches for hers. I thought she just wanted me to join her on this trip to get me out of her system, but she actually needed me here. She needed someone to be the rock while these harsh waves crashed around her. I'm realizing now that there's a lot I don't know about her. I know her body, the way she talks and moves, and the way she ticks. What I don't know is all the history that made her this way, and I desperately seek all of it.

Stirring the two cups of hot chocolate that sit before me, I take both in hand and head onto the balcony, handing one to Indigo.

"Thank you," she says and takes a sip.

I sit on the chair beside hers. Indigo's usual glow to her skin is gone, and she looks paler than normal. The fluffy white blanket which was wrapped around her slides off shoulders. Her emotions are tangible, physically affecting her appearance, and it makes my chest burn.

"Can I ask you a personal question?"

She sips on the hot chocolate before taking a deep breath. "Yes."

"Why do you keep in touch with your family when they're so cruel to you?" I inquire.

"I don't know," she admits, and that surprises me. How can you not know?

I rest a hand on her thigh, gently caressing it. "You know you don't have to put up with that, right? You could cut them off and nobody would think less of you for it."

"I know, but I seek their approval. I seek *her* approval. And it's not always so bad. My mom started going to therapy recently, and although she still has outbursts, she's gotten better."

I frown. "Just because she's trying to do better, doesn't mean you need to put yourself in unhealthy situations while she works on herself. You're her daughter, not her punching bag."

"I know, I know. Alitha and Dahlia tell me all the time."

"You should set some boundaries," I tell her.

"Okay, Simone."

"Huh?"

She laughs and places her cup down on the glass table. "My therapist. She's always talking about boundaries. I started going to her because I think I have an anxiety disorder, and she agrees, but we're still not certain which one yet. It's kind of a new thing."

I smile at her transparency, and she scrunches her nose.

"I graduated from therapy a few years ago," I confess. It's not something I'm sure I've ever told anyone, but if there's ever a time, it feels like it should be now.

"*You* went to therapy? And *graduated*? Damn, I must be in the kindergarten phase."

My brows scrunch. "What—did you not expect that? All graduating therapy means is that I've learned the strategies necessary, and at least for now, I don't need a clinician."

"I guess that makes sense. You just seem so... perfect? Hot?" she says teasingly.

"There's a reason the phrase is hot and bothered," I say with a smirk.

She punches my shoulder. It's barely a tap, but it's cute.

"Don't think that I'm perfect. I mean, you *can* think that, but I hope you know that I come with my own set of baggage too," I say. "I'm obsessive, addicted to working out, and my sex drive is naturally higher than humans."

"I know, I know. But literally nothing you listed was negative. Try again." She giggles and rolls her eyes. We're speaking in jest, but she's still guarded. Arms crossed, there's a level of openness I can't seem to get her to reach with me. Maybe if I open up more, she'll feel comfortable enough to do the same. I want to be that person for her.

"I used to struggle with depression. And abandonment issues. That's what I went to therapy for." I shrug. I still struggle with the abandonment part, but that truth remains unsaid. I don't want to pressure Indigo into making this real because she feels sorry for me. I want her to make this real because she can't stand the thought of me being with someone other than her. Because I can't stand that thought right now either.

"I'm sorry." She places her hand on my cheek, softly cupping it.

"Can I hold you?"

"Please."

Beige limbs tangle with mine as I hold Indigo closely, her face resting against my chest. She snores softly, and I kiss her forehead as my eyelids grow heavy. *Goodnight, little rabbit.*

nine
INDIGO

Stretching out my arms, I look down at Vega, who is still sound asleep. She's drooling on the pillow, but in a sexy way? In the sexiest way that someone can drool.

I need to fucking text the Unholy Trilogy. Snaking my arm over V, I grab my phone off the nightstand, unplugging it from the charger.

> **Indigo**
> Hey, okay, so… I asked Vega to be my holidate for Gratefulness Week.

> **Dahlia**
> Mmmhmmm.

> **Alitha**
> Dahlia told me…

> **Indigo**
> TORRES?!

> **Dahlia**
> In my defense, she was going to find out anyway.

Indigo
Urgh, whatever. Okay, is there a way we're like… destined to be?

Dahlia
Cosmically or biologically?

Indigo
Both? Either?

Dahlia
Do you know her chart????

Indigo
Not really. I know she's a Taurus sun and moon.

Dahlia
Hmmmmmmmmm.

Indigo
This whole thing feels like an illusion, except she never dissipates. She's toooo perfect for me.

Alitha
I could do some research in the lab. See if there's a scientific explanation for all of this.

Dahlia
Omg, YES!!!

Alitha
I just need a small sample of her DNA.

Dahlia
Is she sleeping now? Pull out a strand of her hair or something.

> **Indigo**
> ...

> **Alitha**
> It would be much less risky to just get some from her hair brush.

> **Dahlia**
> True, true.

> **Indigo**
> I'M NOT GIVING YOU BIZZARE BITCHES A HAIR SAMPLE.

> **Alitha**
> That's Dr. Bizarre Bitch to you.

> **Dahlia**
> I just snorted.

I lock my phone and carefully get up, not wanting to wake Vega. She looks like a green cherub, her skin shimmering in the early light of the rising sun. I grab my toiletries out of my suitcase and head for the bathroom. Reaching one arm into the shower, I turn the water on and undress as I wait for it to get hot.

Nobody texted me. Not my mother. Not my father. Not my sister. The Unholy Trilogy replied, of course, but nobody from last night, my own family, dared to see how I'm doing or apologize for their awful behavior. Whatever. I can't let them ruin this week, or let the panic take me. There's a gorgeous woman in the bed I got to sleep in last night, and I won't let anyone ruin that for me.

The warm water washes away my troubles, as it always does. I regret not packing purple shampoo. Dahlia is gonna kick my ass by the end of this week. Maybe I could get some at a store nearby? I'll put that on the to-do list, which was recently updated.

On my to-do list:

- Decorate for Christmas
- Get Vega out of my system
- Buy purple shampoo

Not on my to-do list:

- Developing feelings for my boss
- Waiting for an apology from my mother that'll never come

I'm not doing a great job at the not-list, but I'm trying.

I brush through my hair, detangling it gently. It's Gratefulness Week, dammit. Instead of being miserable and spending the day sulking about my family, I'd rather find something to be grateful for—like fucking the sexy orc that's lying down in the other room. After giving my body a solid 3 rounds of scrubbing, I turn off the water and look at myself in the mirror. It's time to put on the ritz.

Getting out my blow dryer, I consider making a potion that would permanently render it silent, but decide to charm it quiet instead. Butt-naked, I stand there, drying my bob. Throwing on some winged eyeliner, I add the final touch of my signature deep purple lipstick, and shimmer into the bra and panties that Dahlia made me pack. They're lacey and black, and I think now's a better time than ever to put them to good use.

I exit the bathroom and cross towards the kitchen,

where I dig around for ingredients. We don't have much here to make breakfast, so I add that to my mental list. Turning, I suddenly feel her warm body behind me.

"You moved so fast, I hadn't even realized you woke up," I say.

"I was slow until I saw what you were wearing," V whispers in my ear, her voice still groggy from recently waking.

She turns me around, pushing me onto the kitchen counter. The morning sun settles in through the window, lighting the space, and I close my eyes as she nips my neck with her tusks. Vega leaves a trail of wet, heady kisses, before putting her nose up to mine and looking me straight in the eyes.

"I brought you a surprise; do you trust me?"

"Yes," I say, my voice coming out breathy.

She moves away from the counter and crosses towards the bedroom. As she walks away, I get the best view of her solid ass and thighs. She's all muscle, yet somehow has the most delightful bubble butt I've ever seen. It's too perfect. I'm practically drooling as I wait for her to return.

"Close your eyes."

I smile and obey. "Closed them."

Her footsteps come closer, until she's right up against me. Her deeper, sultry voice comes out again. "Open your legs, little rabbit."

A shiver hits my entire body at those words, and I do as I'm told. I'm hoping I'll be rewarded for how good I've been about following her orders.

She places something against my underwear, right on my clit, and I hear a click.

Zzz

Is that a fucking vibrator?

Zzzzzzz.

"Oh my god," I gasp out in pleasure, allowing the feeling to take over me. Vega's tusks run against my neck, and she sucks on my skin, her wet warm mouth dissolving any semblance of control I ever had. I have been stuck in this limbo between wanting to get her out of my system and not wanting to catch feelings, and at this moment I've decided I don't fucking care.

One of V's hands strokes my thigh while the other grabs my hair, exposing my neck further. I'm moaning and enjoying myself when my brain starts doing the math. What's holding up the vibrator?

I shift my head, looking straight into those pools of gold she has for eyes. "How're you doing that?"

"Magic," she says with a wink. Oh my—she can use her hands for other things.

Vega licks all the way down my neck and unhooks my bra. She places my breast into her mouth, sucking on the hard peak of my nipple.

"I can use my tongue," she says, swirling it around again. She flicks one wrist out, pointing up with her finger, and the vibration increases in intensity. "Or I could use my magic."

I'm on the edge when she lowers the setting of the vibrator to almost nothing. I whimper, wanting the pleasure to return.

V kisses me deeply. "Can I charm your body? I have something I want to try on you."

"Right now? You can use me as you see fit."

"Good girl." She kisses me once more, and parts from between my legs. Slipping off her shorts, I can see the short, trimmed black hair and her plump, perfect lips, fully exposed.

Forget anything I ever said about purple. Green is my favorite color.

Vega steps away, rooting for something in one of her bags, and I get a look at her ass. It's the hottest thing I've ever seen. A roundness like a lot of women I've seen, but with the muscle of every star athlete. I can never fuck another human again, knowing what lady orc ass looks like. She places a green dildo onto the counter. It's a deep, fleshy green with olive undertones, similar to the shade of her skin.

Is that for me?

Vega moves her hands, swirling them through the air, and then my hands are locked down onto the counter. The pressure of her magic isn't painful, but it would be incredibly hard to move my arms right now. If I weren't magical, it would be impossible. Even still, her magic greatly outweighs mine in this department. She deserves her title of Department Chair of Charms. *Don't think about work, Indigo*.

I blink, watching as Vega climbs onto the island in the middle of the kitchen. Her hair has been thrown into a bun, and I can see the shaven parts that wrap around underneath. Everything about her is painstakingly sexy. From the nose piercing, to the tattoo on her arm, to the muscles sparkling in the morning sunlight. Everything.

Opening her legs, V puts herself on full display before me. She places two fingers into her mouth, sucking on them before slowly drawing them out and moving them down her lips. She trails down her chin, past her sports bra, and down her chiseled stomach, until she reaches her pussy.

Vega teases at her folds before finally pushing them inside. She moans out in pleasure, and I would do anything to touch her right now. To be touched by her.

As if sensing my need, she uses her other hand to fling her magic out, driving the setting of the small, bullet shaped vibrator all the way up. My legs are shaking, hanging off the counter across from her, but my arms won't move—can't move.

"Vega," I say as she dips her fingers in and out. The sounds of her body opening up is driving me mad. I'm so incredibly close when she snaps her fingers, and the vibrations come to a complete stop.

"You bitch," I say, out of breath and overwrought. I half-mean it.

"Tsk tsk. Talk to me like that, and you'll get nothing, little rabbit."

She reaches back, grabbing the dildo. It is thicker and longer than any I've ever purchased, with a suction cup at the end. She sticks it straight onto the black and white marble she's seated on, and gets up onto her knees. As she lowers herself onto the cock, I watch, mouth agape and watering.

Her body takes it so well. Every muscle in her leg flexes at different moments as she moves herself up and down. Her hands grasp her knees, and I squirm, desperately trying to move my hands out from the force of her magic so I can touch her—touch myself, really.

She moans, biting her lips as she stares into my eyes, and I realize this is the most intimacy I've ever had with someone. I've fucked, I've been fucked, but I've never shared this type of vulnerability, or experienced this level of unadulterated lust, with anyone.

V bounces, the movements quickening, and I whimper, needing to chase the high of my own pleasure.

"Beg for it." It is not a suggestion, but a command. Her voice is liquid gold. "Beg, and I'll let you come."

I almost laugh, but when she stares at me with those fierce, lust-filled eyes, I choose to do as I'm told. "P-please."

"I said beg."

"Vega, I want to come," I say, not sure if I sound awkward or sexy.

One of her eyebrows shifts up, and the vibrator starts again for a split second, before shutting off once more.

Were it not for her magic, my body would cave in on itself, my thighs rubbing against each other, craving friction.

"Please, Vega," I start, before realizing I already said that. I pause briefly, my mind sifting through information until I land on the perfect thing. "Dr. Daelor." Her eyes go wide at that. "I need you to make me come. Fuck me, punish me, do whatever you want with me. I'm yours, please let me finish."

She climbs off the counter, grabbing me and throwing me over her shoulder. My body goes limp as her magic ceases its hold on me, and I let her toss me onto the island countertop. Can I add "being thrown around" onto the list of things I'm into?

Vega climbs up onto the island, and I'm suddenly thankful to past-Indigo for renting the fancier condo with the massive kitchen. Spreading my legs open, Vega uses one hand to hold her body up, while she uses the other to tease my opening. The pink, little vibrator is still charmed, pressed against my clit, and she gradually ups the vibration.

V pushes my underwear to the side before curling one strong finger inside me, I experience pure bliss as Vega fucks me with her finger. When I'm alone, I always require at least two, but with Vega's massive and muscled six-foot-six body, one finger is plenty. She bounces backward onto the dildo, fucking herself as she finishes me off.

"Vega, I'm so close," I say.

"Me too," she replies, bouncing with more fervor than ever.

The overwhelming feeling of her muscles body hovering before me, convulsing as she comes. The combined feeling of the curve of her finger and the pulsing vibrations against my clit send me toppling over the edge.

Slowly, she pulls her finger out of me and moves to kiss me. Her lips are soft, and I smile against them.

"It's still early; can we go back to sleep?" I ask.

"Of course, my rabbit." Vega kisses the top of my forehead, and I nuzzle against her chest.

Not *little* rabbit, but *her* rabbit. How I desperately wish that could be true.

ten
INDIGO

I unwrap myself from Vega, and she laughs as I put on a fresh pair of underwear.

"Two pairs in one day, is that a record?" she teases.

"No, definitely not. I think the record is four. I can't wear the pair I had on this morning because *someone* got them soaked."

"*You* soaked them; I just helped," she says with a smirk.

"Anyways. We need lunch and to run a couple of errands."

"Sure thing. What do you need?"

I start counting on one finger. "Groceries, purple shampoo, new parents."

"Can't help you with the last one. Let's grab a bite, get your shampoo, and hit up groceries last. If I go grocery shopping on an empty stomach, I'll buy everything in the store."

"I feel that."

V's smile is addictive, and I savor her toothy grin. I put on a pair of black leggings, and a black peplum top with wide flared sleeves. Vega is wearing beige cargo pants and a brown sweatshirt with the Augury University logo on it. The embroidered AU is gold, with a dainty golden wreath wrapped around it in a circle. Underneath the AU, are two hands performing magic. It's beautiful, really, I can't think of another University with a cooler logo, but it's a bit on the nose? We're supposed to be hiding that we work there, not making it more obvious.

"Should you change?" I suggest, unsure of how she'll react.

"Meh. Alumni wear this kind of stuff all the time, plus my hair will be up. Nobody is going to think either of us are professors, we're a bit young," she says with utter certainty.

I wish I could live in her head. Curl up next to that pretty brain of hers and cease to feel the anxiety that spirals within my own.

I forget that we're young. I mean, I know I'm young, but Vega is also only twenty-eight. Alitha is twenty-nine, and I believe Malik is in his late twenties as well. Many of the other professors are in their thirties and forties, but some are literally hundreds of years old. We're infants in comparison. My sister's accomplishments made my job at Augury University look frivolous, but I have to remember how amazing this opportunity is and that I cannot fuck it up. I will not get fired because of my unbridled lust for my boss. This week will get her out of my head for good. This is just an itch I have to scratch.

Kissing Momiji on the head, we turn on the TV. The white, fluffy sugar rabbit has his wings wrapped around Freja, who stares intently at the screen. I didn't know hummingmouse were such big fans of reality TV, but I guess if you're going to watch trashy television, Magically Mine is where it's at.

Hopping into the car, we drive towards the center of Octopus Island. The Isles of Magia are all unique in their own ways. Magia Island is full of magic, and the people there are one with nature. We didn't destroy jungles to make our buildings, we built them in the trees, or on open planes. Naiad Island has its own vibe as well, comprised of merfolk cultures from all over the galaxy. Sleeping Island is a quieter place, and a more tight-knit community. They've dedicated a lot of resources into archiving and preserving humanities' culture from before The Convergence. Octopus Island is the odd man out. The name derives from the creatures that lurk in waters around it, but the island itself is anything but friendly to nature. On Turtle Island, in The Americas, there is a region in the west known as the Valleys of Silicon. It's a hyper-technological space. Octopus Island is similar, utilizing more technology than magic.

After The Convergence, humanity had to rebuild. Most of our ancestors banded together with the magical races, combining nature with magic, magic with science, and science with technology to forge a new world. There's a balance we've carefully struck, but some pockets of the globe have decided other methods were better. They allowed technology to take over. I think it's one of the ways that humans, the ones without magic, feel in control. Either way, there's a lot of debate in the political sphere on how much of that technology is safe, but ultimately we cannot govern communities that are not our own.

I watch Vega as we drive to the main city, her brows remaining furrowed the entire time. She's seeing it too—

seeing what I hate about this place. How clear it is that they cut down trees and manipulated the Earth to create this place.

Though I was raised on Octopus Island, I spent my entire life dreaming of anything else. It felt... uncomfortable. There's something about feeling the grass against my feet that is so natural and grounding, and Octopus Island is nearly void of that. There is grass, sure, but it is perfectly contained in little suburbs.

As we drive past pristine house after pristine house, the anxious feeling in my gut heightens. I am being reminded of how much I hate it here—reminded of how much Magia Island has become my home. I've been living there for eight years now, ever since I was accepted to Augury University after I graduated high school early. I thank my lucky stars for Augury, for it has become my home.

We park the car on a side chute of Main Street, and I hop out of the car. Tapping my phone against the meter, I pay the four dabloons it costs to park for the day.

Vega looks at me with a peculiar expression. "It costs money to park here?"

I shrug. "Yep. This place sucks, dude."

"Okay, okay. Take a deep breath," she says, and so I do, letting out a deep sigh. "I know you hate it here and you want to be miserable and for me to commiserate with you, but I don't want to. You invited me to come out with you. Let's treat this like we're random tourists. Ignore all the capitalist-technological-hellscape parts of this island, and let's just enjoy the holiday and each other's company."

"I'm sorry. You're right," I say.

"It's okay. You have bad memories from this place,

and it isn't as magic-friendly as you'd prefer. I get it, I really do, but let's make the best of it. Focus on the good stuff, like the fact that they're decorating this place for all the winter holidays," she says, taking my hand in hers.

We walk down the busy street, and it reminds me of why I love this season. There are people putting up Christmas lights, wreaths for Winter Solstice, and light fixtures shaped into the Star of David. As we pass a family, I see a poster in a woman's arms that reads "POETRY READING FOR YALDĀ NIGHT." So many cultures, so many planets, and yet nearly all people have their own way of celebrating winter.

We walk towards a hair supply store.. Vega goes to open the door, when a small crowd of people come marching towards us holding pamphlets.

Are they all... religious? Is this a cult? Some type of spell? I honestly have no idea what is going on, but they're all wearing funny outfits that remind me of old movies.

Vega's eyes widen, and her eyebrows scrunch like she's just deciphered what's going on. "They're Christmas Carolers... in November."

The party of people, mostly human but a few cambion, elves, and hybrids take in a collective breath.

"Dashing through the snow," a woman's voice sings out.

"In a one-horse open sleigh," a man joins.

"O'er the hills we go." Each line is like a solo, and I can't help but grin.

"Laughing all the way."

A child jumps out from behind their parents. "Ha. Ha. Ha."

I take Vega by the hand and lead her into the store as

the singers continue down the street, coming up to all who pass.

"That was… prematurely festive," I say with a small laugh. Vega and I continue down the isles until we find the one dedicated to white hair. Every section is broken down by hair color, then texture, then product. "What was that?" I ask as I grab the purple bottle. Though my hair is naturally white, if I don't use a special shampoo, it often looks brassy. This shampoo helps the lavender tint to last longer.

V tilts her head at me. "The Christmas Carolers?"

"Is there some kind of event going on?"

She shrugs, not answering as we approach the checkout counter. An employee rings me up in polite silence, and we cross the threshold to exit the store.

Vega looks at me. "This is your hometown, you tell me. Is there usually some kind of event during this time?"

I roll my eyes. "I haven't lived here in forever. I just think it's weird that they'd celebrate so early."

Vega laughs as we continue down the street towards a sandwich shop. "People always celebrate Christmas early. I think it's hilarious. It's humanity's thing, I don't know. Did you not celebrate Christmas growing up?"

"We do. My dad loves Christmas, but my mom was always more into Winter Solstice. I think she just likes the aesthetics of Christmas, since none of us are religious."

"That's funny. My mom celebrated a Barac holiday called Jul—"

"God rest ye, merry Gentlemen," a caroler sings, interrupting Vega.

What is going on?

"Didn't we just fucking see carolers?" I whisper through gritted teeth.

People walk by and stop to watch. There's a mother orc carrying her toddler son, and he watches in awe of the vocalists.

"I think these are the same people too," Vega whispers back. She takes me by the hand, snaking me out of the small crowd that's forming, and we head back down the street.

"God rest ye, merry mouths," I say once everyone is out of earshot.

Vega lets out a grunt of a laugh, and my cheeks turn red.

The carolers are continuing this direction, and I'm getting rather annoyed by them. "Why don't we go somewhere else instead of the sandwich shop?"

"That's fine with me," Vega says. "Anything you had in mind?"

"There's a ramen and boba place two streets over," I suggest and she squeezes my hand.

"Lead the way."

Crossing Main Street towards Token Bubbles, there are workers putting up holiday decorations at every corner. Lots of specialized screens that flash different designs for a multitude of holidays.

"You were telling me about Jul? It sounds like Yule," I say, passing a bookstore and a crystal shop.

"It's similar in many ways. Orcs would eat these animals... similar to boars, and we'd light candles and tell stories around a fire. When I was young, and my mother was still around, we did an earthly version of it with hot chocolate. I can recall sitting in her lap, snow on the ground, and we were bundled up around the fire pit," Vega shares, and my heart sinks. Although my family is awful at times, they're alive. They are a phone call away.

I pull her hand up to my face and kiss it gently. We continue walking until we're at the doors of Token and Bubbles and step inside.

There is a beautiful mural of a wave painted on the wall as we get in line.

"Could I please get grilled chicken ramen with extra chicken? And a brown sugar milk tea," Vega says. Her voice is smooth and warm, with a deep timbre.

I order the same, without all the extra chicken, and some kind of passion fruit drink with popping pearls that sounds appealing.

Walking up to the machine to pay, Vega bumps me out of the way with her hip and places her phone on top of the machine.

"As the person who gets to decide if you deserve a pay raise, you deserve a fucking pay raise *and* a free meal" Vega whispers to where no one can hear, and I flush.

"Vega, I make the base adjunct pay, which is not bad at all. I can pay for myself."

"You are doing more than any other adjunct, and frankly more than many of the other professors. Don't argue with me; I'm paying for your food."

I sigh and accept. I hate to say this, but I love it when she's bossy. When men tell me what to do, it makes me want to scream, but when Vega does it, something melts inside me. I immediately want to abide. Maybe I should bring this up in therapy too. Bisexuality is strange. Sometimes it feels like my personality alters a little, depending on the gender of my partner. But Vega isn't my partner.

The server calls our number.

"Do you want to sit outside? The weather is really beautiful out," I suggest.

"Not as beautiful as you."

I roll my eyes. "Has that line ever worked on *anyone*?"

"It just did." She winks. "Yeah, let's eat outside."

Grabbing the tray, Vega and I open the door that leads to the patio outside. The air is slightly chilled, and it's refreshing. We sit down, and I watch as Vega takes a massive bite of chicken.

"Can I ask a silly question out of ignorance? I'm just seeking to understand you better," I say nervously. I hate asking people—monsters, humans, anyone—of different cultures or from other planets questions about why they do things. They don't owe me anything, but I want to know everything about everyone. It fascinates me. Admittedly, I'm also terrified I'll come across as rude or insensitive.

"Go for it."

"I've noticed... orcs eat a lot of meat? Like, a lot more meat than humans. Is there a reason for that?" I ask.

Vega's golden eyes shimmer back at me. "That's not something we're sensitive about, so don't worry. Our bodies simply demand more protein. It's one of the reasons orcs are naturally more muscular."

"Deck the halls with boughs of holly, fa, la, la, la, la, la, la, la, la." There is a group of voices singing, and the sound of marching footsteps from around the corner.

"Are you kidding me? Did you pay these people to follow us?" I ask V as they get closer to the restaurant.

Vega smirks, one corner of her mouth perking up. "No, but I wish I orchestrated this. It would make this one hundred times funnier."

They continue singing as they walk, until the carolers are standing directly in front of the patio. There's only a few other people on the deck, and everyone seems to be amazed by the singers. Everyone but me, apparently.

I don't know whether to laugh or scream when they all open up their coats and take out a plethora of hats. From Santa hats to elf ears, everyone sticks something on their head.

"Isn't it kind of weird that people still dress up as Christmas elves, when actual elves exist?"

"Yeah, a bit. I think they call them something else now... Santa's fae? Something like that," Vega says as the carolers continue. "Most elves are so tall, they don't look anything like Santa's helpers."

"Except my elfborn family. We inherited so many elven traits, except the height."

Vega's smirk widens into the biggest grin I've ever seen on her. "They should cast you guys next time."

"I'm going to kill you."

"Sh!" A human woman shushes me, and I look at V with wide eyes.

We continue eating our ramen in silence, the sound of Christmas music grating in my ears. There's no place I'd rather be than here with Vega, being tortured by Christmas carolers, day dreaming about a future we might never have together because of stupid fucking work policies. I wish I didn't love my job so much.

Maybe in another life I'm an assassin, or a restaurant worker, or an engineer like my mother wanted me to be. Vega could still work as a professor. Maybe in another life, I'm hers.

eleven
INDIGO

P*ING*.

"What was that?" I say with a yawn.

Ping.

"It's your phone; it's been blowing up for like a half-hour," Vega says as she turns in bed to face me. I'm bleary eyed and groggy, but I'm awake. Vega's face is stiff, like she slept with it smushed into a pillow the entire night, and I giggle.

"Should I check it?"

I unlock my phone to a plethora of texts from my mother.

> **Mom**
> Indigo, will we be seeing you today?
>
> I'm so sorry

> Indigo, I have to apologize for the other night. My medication had worn off and I've been very stressed lately. I know it's not an excuse, but my therapist and I talked about it, and I wanted to tell you I really didn't mean most of what I said. I mean I did, but I didn't. I usually mean what I say, but not how I say it.

> We are getting the Christmas tree this morning at 10. Do not miss it.

> That sounded very bossy, but it's family tradition. Your father would be very upset if you weren't there.

> I'm not trying to be annoying, but could you answer the phone? What if something happened to you? Don't make your poor mother worry.

"Fucking hell on Earth, what is her problem?" Vega says from over my shoulder.

I sigh, typing up a single response.

> **Indigo**
> We will be there to get the tree.

"Is she always like this? Or did something recent make it worse?" Vega inquires.

"I mean, yes, and yes. The holidays are especially triggering for her, but this is pretty much the norm. She has good days and bad days–times where she hurts me, and times where she helps."

Vega's mouth twists to the side, and her septum piercing moves as her nostrils flare. "I don't even know how to respond. How do you deal with this all the time?"

"Not sure. I think it's easier because I moved away.

Sometimes I just mute her number for a few weeks. Other times, she's so busy with Iris that she forgets to text me. It's a weird dichotomy."

Vega sits up, pushing the blanket off of her. "So, where are we going?"

"Raemond Hill—it's a plant nursery that imports Christmas trees. We go every year. We're supposed to be there in forty-five minutes, so we better hurry up and get dressed."

"Do you want me to make breakfast?" Vega offers, standing up in just her boxer-briefs and a sports bra.

"I don't think we have time. Maybe we can get smoothies on the way back and then I'll make us lunch?"

"I'd like to cook for you," Vega says.

"Okay," I say, cheeks flushed pink. She always wants to take care of me, and if I'm being honest with myself, I always want to let her.

Momiji and Freja are flying across the room, racing one another, when I put out a bowl of lettuce and carrots for them to chomp on. Freja is significantly faster and makes her way over to the bowl, reaching it before Momiji even lands on the table.

Heading back into the bedroom, I open my suitcase and take out a black sweater and matching leggings. The sweater is knitted, and there are holes in the sleeve where I've shoved my thumb through.

"Vega," I shout.

"Yes, love...ly," she shouts back. There was a long pause between *love* and the *ly* sound at the end, and I can't help fixate on it. Part of my brain wants to ball it up and toss it into a fire and burn it, never to be uttered again. I can't be her love, not now. The other part of me wants to hold it close to my heart. I blink away the thought before an anxiety spiral seizes me.

"Do you think my mom will be mad at me if I show up in a sweater with holes in the sleeve?" I ask.

Vega walks into the room, brows furrowed, and shrugs. "I don't know, and frankly, I do not care—*we* do not care." Vega stops and points to her and I. "Stop caring and wear what you want."

"It's just... it's so comfy."

"You don't have to explain yourself to me. Wear the sweater."

"Alright," I say. "Let's go see my family."

The plant nursery is just as I remember it. There are large black metal gates leading into a wide open space, with lots of potted plants lined up on tables and the ground surrounding them. There is the old section where they keep imported trees, as well as a new section of some sort of pine which is actually growing out of the ground. Magic must be required to grow these trees on Octopus Island.

Entering through the gates, I spot Iris standing next to our parents, who are all in their own unique outfits. Iris is wearing short, orange corduroy overalls on top of a tight, black top, which is so typical for her. If I wore something like that growing up, I'd have been scolded for showing too much leg, but our mom always let Iris wear whatever she wanted. Mom, who always dresses more conservatively, is wearing a long, flowy black top over pants, and our dad is in a t-shirt and jeans. At least dad's outfit is practical. We all look like we're attending different events, and it makes me chuckle a bit to myself.

"You good?" Vega asks as we get out of the SUV and head towards my family.

"Yeah, just thinking."

As we reach my family, my dad pulls me into a hug and kisses my forehead.

"I'm sorry, sweet girl. I should've defended you the other night. You know how your mother can be sometimes," he whispers, and I smile, forcing myself not to let out the tears that threaten to fall.

"So, do we want an imported one, or one of those weird experimental ones growing out of the ground?" Iris asks. "I hear a potion mage created them."

"Well then, in honor of you, our little potion mage, let's get one!" My mom says and starts walking. We all follow after her, crossing by tall trees coming out of the ground, and we head towards the back of the nursery. Vega holds my hand, rubbing my pointer finger with her thumb in an attempt to soothe me.

Coming up the pathway, we stop at a little shack. There are axes hanging from the outer wall, and a short cambion leans against their desk reading a book. The cambion, who I'm almost certain is Raemond in disguise, has massive breasts that are falling out of their shirt. Their high-waisted leather pants lead to chunky black heels. It's ridiculous how sexual they're posed, with their tail waving back and forth.

"Raemond," Iris says with a cough.

The cambion shifts into their usual form, wearing a sweatshirt and biker shorts. Raemond has pinky-red skin and white straight hair cut into a bob. They have short black horns that are spiked, growing out of the top of their head. Although some cambion have wings, Raemond does not.

"Is this more... family friendly?" they ask Iris, who laughs.

"Yeah, who the fuck were you dressed up for anyway?" Iris's smile is wider than I've seen in years, and it sends a pang to my heart.

Raemond adjusts their square-shaped glasses. "There's a guy who buys a lot of his plants here. I don't know his name, but he's very tall and hunky. I saw his car drive by and was hoping to catch his attention, but I guess he didn't stop. Oh well, maybe another time." Raemond lets out a deep sigh. "Or maybe I'll just die alone."

My mouth opens, unsure of what I should say in response to that, but Iris just laughs. Maybe this is an inside joke? Vega's expression is amused as she witnesses this all unfold.

"Was that an illusion?" my dad asks Raemond, breaking the awkward silence.

"It was!" they say, unbothered by their previous statement.

I start to think that my mother is being oddly quiet, when I realize she's no longer standing with us. Looking around, I see she's already investigating the new experimental trees.

Iris, Raemond, and my father head over to Mom, while Vega stands with me by the shack.

"How come you all get your tree here every year?" Vega asks.

"Before Raemond inherited the family business, I think it belonged to their aunt... uncle... ancle? Cambion all have a different thing with gender. Some of them like gendered terms, others don't, but generally they're all what we'd consider genderqueer."

"I feel that." Vega smiles wide. "I'm what they'd call... a little queer."

"A *little*? You're really gay *and* really tall, there's nothing little to you." I shake my head. "Anyway, I think it was their aunt Roxana. We always got our trees here growing up, it's just kind of a tradition. Maybe one day Iris will have a kid, and they'll come here too."

"Vega, would you be a dear and grab an ax?" my mother yells in our direction.

"No need," Vega shouts. "I'll just use my magic."

Raemond snaps their fingers and is suddenly next to us, staring up at us with golden eyes, more yellow than Vega's. "You cannot use magic to cut down these trees; you have to do it by hand."

"That takes so much effort," my dad says, walking our way.

"It takes the same amount of effort it took humans to cut down trees before The Convergence. I'm not trying to be a dick; it's just a rule from the mage who created these trees. You have to do it the old-fashioned way," Raemond explains.

Vega grabs an ax off the wall and throws it over her shoulder, heading back towards my mother and the tree she's selected. My father follows suit. Raemond transforms, their body shifting into a tall, lean and muscular figure. They grab an ax, and we all head to the tree. Although I've known Raemond for a long time, this illusion skill is new, and it's impressive.

Iris is sitting on the ground, watching videos on her phone. I know twenty-four and twenty-two isn't a massive age gap, but she looks like a child to me right now, the way she's so enamored by whatever she's watching. She'll always be my little sister, no matter how hard she tries to be bigger than me.

Vega swings the ax, chopping at the base of the tree. The muscles in her arms flex with every swing, shown off thanks to her tank top. I know that my whole family is next to me, that Raemond is here too, but I don't care. As V chops down that tree, it is just me and her in this whole wide world. I stare at her beautiful lady orc ass and remember how she looks without the sweatpants on.

I am, once again, reminded that green is my new favorite color.

Vega and Raemond carry the massive tree onto the roof of my dad's luxury SUV. You can see my mom wince at every branch which scratches against the top of the vehicle, but my dad doesn't seem to mind. He stares at Vega in awe.

"Dude, I think Dad is more in love with your girlfriend than you are," Iris jests. *More in love with my girlfriend.* I let the words settle in my mouth, but I don't utter another sound.

Once the pine is secured, my mother pulls out her phone and sends Raemond the dabloons she owes them for the tree. Raemond walks back through the gate and waves their hand and tail simultaneously, saying goodbye.

"Are you two close?" Vega asks Iris.

"Yeah! Raemond is in my book club. We read a lot of smut together," Iris says without an ounce of shame. It's kind of amazing how much she's unapologetically herself.

My mom is sneakily trying to take pictures as the three of us are talking, when my dad starts the car. "Come on Ilona, we've got to get home to decorate the tree for Gratefulness Dinner. We only have a few days to prepare the house," he shouts.

"Coming, dear."

She gives Iris and I wet, sloppy kisses on the cheek before hopping into dad's car. *Ick.*

Iris drove herself here, and she gives us a small wave before jumping into her own vehicle. "See ya in a couple days, love birds."

We hop into the car, and Vega looks at me with fervor in her eyes. She leans over my body, her arm hovering above me as she locks my car door, and then grabs my face in her hand and kisses me.

The kiss deepens before I break from it. What is she doing? "Vega, we're in public."

"Did we not just see a half-demon bent over reading smut?" Vega asks, and I stifle a laugh.

"Yes, but there are children who come here, Vega."

"Ugh, fine. You're right." Vega gives me a look, one eyebrow raised. "Smoothies?"

"A smoothie sounds great right now."

The next morning, I was slow to wake, slow to get up, and slow to start the day. Vega and I spent hours in bed snuggling, watching a Christmas movie from every millennium of humanity. We started with the 1900s, and went all the way up until recently, which ended with a movie about a satyr and a cambion falling in love over the holidays.

I didn't ask Vega to take a photo with me this week, mostly because I didn't want to have something to stare at late at night when I'm missing her in the weeks after this trip. I don't want to wallow in what could be. I did, however, sneak a photo of her with Momiji and Freja resting on both of her shoulders. It's from the back, and it's a little blurry, but it's mine. My little keepsake.

I flip to my texts with the Unholy Trilogy and type away as Vega uses the bathroom.

> **Indigo**
> Can someone remind me of why I like my job more than I like Vega?

> **Dahlia**
> Because it pays your bills!! And you get to work with Alitha doing fun magic stufffff?

> **Indigo**
> Yeah...

> **Alitha**
> I'm not sure you do.

> **Indigo**
> :/

twelve

VEGA

Indigo has been brushing her teeth for *six* minutes. I don't know what kind of anxious state she's in, but I think her brain is convinced the more she brushes, the less likely it is that dinner will go poorly.

If anyone ever made me feel this bad, I would probably punch them in the face, I lie to myself. In reality, I'd just block their number. But Indigo, as kind hearted as she is, remains in contact with everyone that hurts her. She's *too* kind. I don't know much about Indie's dating history, but I can imagine if one of her awful ex's came knocking on her door asking for help, she'd let them right in too.

I admire it though, really. When my mother and little brother passed away, my father died along with them. He gave up on me when I needed him most. I could never see Indigo doing that to her family, not even to Iris. As much as the two seem to have issues, I truly believe Indigo would do anything for her sister if it came down to it.

"Indigo, we've got to get going. Dinner is in less than an hour," I say into the crack of the bathroom door.

"I'm coming." Indigo's words are muffled and coated with toothpaste. "Wait in the kitchen for me."

I head into the kitchen, leaning against the island as I adjust my suspenders. I'm clad in solid black, dress pants and top with suspenders and loafers. I look... really fucking good. I hear the pitter patters of what is either Indigo's footsteps or my heart. Maybe both. Typically, I don't get anxious or nervous, but whatever I'm experiencing now is something similar—*butterflies*—as I wait for Indigo to enter the room.

Damn. Besides that time she borrowed my sweater, this is the first I've ever seen her in any color other than black. A deep green velvet, the dress cuts low on her petite chest. Embossed with roses, it's absolutely gorgeous. There's a sort of twisted wrap effect to it, pulling at her hips, accentuating their curve. Indigo is lean-but-hippy, and it shows off her frame well. It's stunning—*she's* stunning.

Mouth agape, I stare at her in awe.

"Well, don't act so shocked," she says. "You make it seem like I look unkempt most of the time."

"I've just never seen you wear anything other than black."

"Oh." She twirls in the dress, showing off. "Green is my favorite color."

I thought it was purple. "Since when?"

"Since you."

Our eyes meet, and there's so much unsaid between us. Her words have implications; they give me hope. I still have a chance at changing our fate.

As we pull up to the Watson house, it's different this time. The eaves and gables of the roof are lined with bright white Christmas lights, and the yard is covered in decorative blow-up snowmen. I can't tell if we're about to walk into a Christmas movie or a Christmas catastrophe. I'm hoping for the former.

Indigo interlocks her fingers with mine as we walk inside. The door swings open to Iris, who invites us in. She's smiling wide, like she always does, and I realize how different she is from Indigo and their mother. Indigo is happy and bubbly, but there's a hesitation in her voice and movements at times. The anxiety leaks out of her, and, while it's endearing, it's also clear that it hurts her. Similarly, there's a sadness in Mrs. Watson. Her smiles don't seem to reach her eyes. But Iris doesn't come across this way. There's no anxiety or melancholia bubbling at the surface. If she has any, she must keep it locked deep down, like I do.

Inside the living room is the pine we picked out together the other day, now covered in lights and ornaments. A few are clearly from when Indigo and Iris were children, and I can't help but stop and stare at the white-haired child with big purple eyes in some of the photos. She was always adorable.

"Come sit at the table, everyone; dinner's almost ready," Mrs. Watson shouts from the kitchen. There's a cinnamon smell coming from her direction, and it's enticing me to want whatever she's cooking. I'm practically drooling, I'm so hungry.

We all walk into the dining room and take our seats. Indigo's father is dressed up, just as we are, but Iris didn't get the memo. She's in an oversized anime t-shirt and a black mini-skirt. To each their own, but I can't imagine wearing something like that in front of my own father. I'd receive a lecture, even at twenty-eight.

"Did you get Mom anything for Christmas yet?" Iris whispers to Indigo, who is seated next to me.

"Not yet; why?" Indigo whispers back.

"I was thinking we could go halfsies and get her and Dad a cruise."

Indigo stares at their father, then back at Iris. "Dude?"

Iris rolls her eyes. "He already knows. The surprise is for Mom, dip-ass."

I try not to interject their sisterly bickering, though it pains me. I guess it's something I'll never understand.

"So, Vega, tell me about your job," Mr. Watson inquires.

My job? Fucking hell, they don't know I work at Augury. Job—what did we say I do? I have zero memory. Play it cool, Vega. "Well, I get to use my magic quite often."

"Oh really? How so?" he asks.

I remember my conversation with Indigo. Her parents can't know that I work at Augury, but I need to impress her mother with my magic... but what did we decide I do? "It really comes in handy. Of course, anyone can work in almost any field, but my magic definitely makes it easier for me."

I'm an idiot. I really just mage-splained the usefulness of magic to a human married into a magical family. Jeez. I've never been off my game more than today.

"Not to be weird, but I've always wondered this. Do

people's sweat make the equipment fall apart faster?" he asks, and I blanche. Sweat? Equipment? Did we tell them I design sex toys for a living?

"I'm not sure," I say, seeking an out from this conversation. By the looks of Iris' tongue sticking out and Indigo's snarl, I'd say they're still getting into it with one another.

"With a body like yours, I'm sure your customers believe you know what you're doing," he says. "You'll have to give me pointers sometime. As you can see, I'm rusty."

That's... so incredibly perverted. And strange. Why would he say that? Indigo is so lucky that I adore her, because otherwise I'd walk out.

"I—"

"Yeah!" Iris interrupts. "I never really thought Indigo would be into a muscle mommy, but here we are."

Muscle mommy? *Oh.* I really am an idiot.

"Who better to design gym equipment than an expert at working out?" Indigo says with a grin, leaning closer to me.

I have never been so embarrassed in my life. I'm so flustered, I think my ancestors on Barac can feel it in the past. If my skin weren't green, it would be flushed bright red right now.

"Everything okay?" Indigo whispers, her lips brushing against my ear.

"Just peachy," I say and place a hand on her thigh. I can never tell her about this, she wouldn't let me live it down.

"Dinner's ready," Mrs. Watson says jovially, carrying a tray with one hand, while using her magic to carry in the others. All at once plates come down onto the table.

There's turkey, mashed potatoes, salad, and even lasagne.

Mr. Watson cuts into the meat, passing it around the table until everyone's plate is full of food. I love food, and as excited I am to eat all of this, I can't help wondering where the cinnamon scent went.

"I'm so glad you could join us, Vega, truly," Mrs. Watson starts. I can visibly see Indigo tense up at the statement. "Sometimes we worry that Indigo and Iris won't find love, but I'm happy to see she's having some success in her romantic life."

"Huh?" Worried for what? They're both beautiful, both young, and both successful. How would Indigo or Iris have any problems dating?

"Indie hasn't had a serious partner since undergrad. You're the first person she's brought home to us in years," Mrs. Watson shares, and my heart throbs.

First person she brings home, and it's not even real. Well, it's real to me, just maybe not to her.

"Iris has never really had an interest in anyone." Mr. Watson frowns. "At least not anyone real."

"Why would I set myself up to be disappointed? Fictional men are better anyways," Iris jokes, but I get the sense that she's not exactly kidding.

"As you can see, they're both worrisome," Mrs. Watson says and takes a big bite of turkey.

I think the problem I have with people like Mrs. Watson is that Indigo and Iris don't need to find love. I want them to, especially Indigo, if that's what they want, but it's not required. You can live a full life without romance. Without sex. Everyone's needs and desires are different, and it's weird of her to push her personal expectations onto her daughters.

Mrs. Watson flicks her wrist, and Christmas music starts to play. Some recently released popular Christmas melody comes on, and the singers take it away. Indigo stares at me, completely frozen, until I snap my fingers in front of her eyes.

Coming out of it, she shakes her head. "Sorry, I was thinking about those Christmas carolers."

"Christmas carolers, are you talking about the group that walks around Main Street? I've been thinking about joining them. Maybe next year," Mrs. Watson shares, and I take a bite of lasagne. The flavors are rich, and I'm glad, because I was about to open my mouth when I shouldn't.

"Of course," Indigo says. "You would join the most annoying group known to man."

"C'mon, Indie, you and I both know the most annoying group ever was that craft club Mom ran when I was in middle school," Iris shares.

"Craft club?" I ask.

"It was an arts club." Mrs. Watson crosses her arms, appearing humorless.

"They really created art. One time, Mom cut our sandwiches to look like dinosaurs." Iris laughed. "Except mine fell apart—"

"And mine looked like a dick. Everyone made fun of me, and I had a panic attack and went home crying." Though Indigo is sharing something that sounds awful, her smile and laughter is genuine, which warms my heart. I've been a little afraid to joke about trauma with her, but she seems to be opening up to it.

Mr. Watson scratches the back of his neck. "I had to pick her up early from school that day. I couldn't understand why she was crying until she showed me my wife's dick sandwiches."

"Alright, alright. Thanks a lot, Emilio. I get it; I'm terrible at arts and crafts," Mrs. Watson says, her tone defeated.

This is a normal amount of family drama. A healthy amount. I hope all of Indigo's future Gratefulness Dinner's are like this, and I hope I get to see them....

"Did you guys know that although Gratefulness Week is a tradition the satyrs brought over from their planet, humans used to celebrate a similar holiday called Thanksgiving Day?" Mr. Watson shares.

"Yeah, but wasn't it like... a colonizer holiday? Or like, it had some kind of awful origin story," Iris says.

I shrug. I actually don't know. I've never heard of 'Thanksgiving.'

"Yeah, the origins were definitely not favorable. The holiday, alongside the Fourth of July, were pretty much wiped away with The Convergence, especially since Turtle Island and Abya Yalla came together to form The Americas," Indigo explains. I love her brain.

"Well, then I'm glad the satyr holiday took over. It's a whole week long too! Which is great. A nice break from school and work for everyone," Mr. Watson says. Indigo makes a funny face, but I think she decides to let it go once her mom gets up.

"Who wants apple pie?" Mrs. Watson offers, and I just about leap out of my seat.

"Before dessert, let's all share something we're grateful for." Mr. Watson looks around the room, and there's a plethora of reactions. I probably look like I want to strangle the man, Indigo is a polite-neutral, and Iris is beaming.

"I'll start," he says. "I'm grateful for my beautiful wife and our two lovely daughters."

There's a pang in my chest. I wonder if my father is thinking of me.

"I'm grateful for fanfiction, chocolate peanut butter cups, and wifi," Iris says. "Oh, and my... magical discovery."

Mrs. Watson looks full of pride. "I'm grateful for Iris, who has stopped cancer from coming back after it goes into remission." She takes a deep breath. "And for Indigo, who is making her own discoveries at her own pace."

Can this woman say one nice thing without making it a slight against her poor daughter?

"What about you, Vega?" Mr. Watson asks.

That's too easy. "I'm grateful for apple pie and Indigo Watson."

thirteen

INDIGO

THE FERRY HOME IS A QUIET TRIP. I LEAN MY BACK AGAINST Vega, whose arms wrap around me as we silently watch the sunset at the edge of the waters. The sky is a bright red, and I recall the old adage my dad used to say to me. *Red sky morning, sailor's warning; red sky night, sailor's delight.*

I've missed home. On Octopus Island, the stars aren't visible. There's too many lights everywhere. But on Magia? Almost every star in the sky can be seen, especially in the Illusionary Jungle. I'm glad to be back, truly, but the reality dawns on me that our week of holidating is over. We can't remain lovers, so are we friends? Does she just become my boss now? I thought I was getting her out of my system, but now that feels like the furthest thing from the truth. I'm addicted to her.

Images of every scenario possible flash through my mind. The two of us dating, only to be caught and forced to break up. Dean Bariel finding out and firing me—firing Vega. There are a hundred terrible ways this could all play out.

Exiting the ferry, we head towards the parking garage in tense silence. Once you give so much of yourself to someone, it's hard to reel it back in.

I pop open my trunk, and Vega places my suitcase inside.

I face away from V. I can't look her in the eyes right now. "I guess I'll see you at work tomorrow," I say, not wanting to let the emotions out. If I say anything more, I might tumble down like a house of cards.

She grabs me by the hips and gracefully spins me around, pulling me close. Our lips collide, and I allow my muscles to relax, my body melting into hers.

Vega takes her mouth off mine, but keeps her hands on my waist.

"We're not done," she says quietly. It's not a warning, but a promise.

"Vega, the university's policy—"

"I know the policy, Indigo. I'm not saying we should break the rules, I'm just reminding you that we agreed to holidate, which is not dating. We're simply each other's plus ones for this holiday season."

My forehead creases as I try to wrap my brain around her implications. "So, what now? Gratefulness week is over."

"And it's going to be December," she interrupts me. "Christmas and Jul and Winter Solstice—all of the best holidays—are coming. I went on a whole trip for your holidate, allow me one holidate of my own."

"You want one date?"

"*Holidate*," she corrects me. "I want one final hoorah. You said you needed to get me out of your system. Let me coarse through it properly, first."

"Okay," I agree, because she's right. This week did *not*

get her out of my system, but maybe we just weren't trying hard enough. I'm deluding myself into thinking one last date, or fuck, might just do the trick. My mind spins through everything that could go wrong again, but I shove that feeling back down. "When?"

"Saturday?" she suggests, and I nod.

"Saturday."

We have to unloop our familiar's, who are wrapped around one another, refusing to separate, before saying goodbye. Her tusks brush against my skin as she kisses my forehead and then turns back to her car.

Unlocking the front door, Momiji and I enter the house, my suitcase heavy in my arms, but not as heavy as my heart feels. I fumble with my keys, almost dropping my bag, but use my magic to stop it from hitting the floor. My body is exhausted; this past week was a mess. Between my mother's mood swings and the lack of permanence between Vega and I, I think this little vacation only made me feel worse about everything. And I can't forget about Iris. I still feel like we haven't resolved anything either.

Slouching on the couch, I get out my phone to text the Unholy Trilogy.

> **Indigo**
> Just got home!

I turn on the TV as I wait for their reply. Momiji flies over to me, his white fluffy body in contrast with the dark purple of the sofa, and we snuggle up to one another.

Ping.

Dahlia
How was it?

Indigo
Eh. My mother was having a really rough day the first time we saw them, but everything was fine for the most part.

Dahlia
What kind of rough day??

Indigo
She was kinda a bully :/

Dahlia
I'm sorry, Watson. I'll kick her ass if you want.

Indigo
I wish, lol.

Alitha
How was Dr. Daelor?

Dahlia
OHYMGOD don't call her that.

Indigo
She was great. Toooooooo great. We're going on one final date this Saturday.

Alitha
Sure you are.

It really will be the final date. I have to draw a line in the sand, I can't lose my fucking job over a hot woman. A brilliant, emotionally intelligent, wonderful fucking woman... but still.

This week is finals week at Augury University, and I can't help but wonder how my students are going to do. I taught history during grad school, and, while the students did well, this is my first year as an adjunct where I'm also teaching charms…. If I'm being honest with myself, I don't feel very confident in the subject. I've always been better with potions, as crazy as that sounds. I try not to dwell on the past more than my silly brain already requires, but sometimes I regret not majoring in potions. I think if my mother was going to be disappointed in me no matter what, I could have at least made it count.

My eyes flutter until they close, and my mind drifts into darkness.

Crash.

What the fuck was that?

My body flings itself off the couch, and I race towards the kitchen, where I find nothing. Coming back into the living room, I finally see it. There's broken glass on the floor behind the couch, liquid coating the floor. Momiji is sprawled across my potion shelf with not one fuck to give.

"Why would you knock off one of my potions? You're lucky that was one that's easy to reproduce," I say in a stern voice.

Momiji moves his foot towards another potion, and I move to grab at him. His wings shoot out, pushing potions over in their wake, and he flies around the room. I somehow manage to catch three potions, the fourth stopped mid-fall by my magic. What a little shit. Did I do something to piss him off? He must be hungry or something...

Putting the potions back on the shelf, I cross towards the kitchen where I open the fridge and get out the carrots. We're almost out, and some of the lettuce looks bad. I'll have to go grocery shopping after work tomorrow. I place a carrot onto my cutting board and reach for the knife drawer. Turning back, Momiji is seated in front of me, one potion between his paws.

"What is your problem?" I shout in frustration, and the sugar rabbit makes a pouty face at me. "Do you want to drink the potion or something?"

He shakes his head.

"Do you... want me to work on my potions more?"

Momiji nods, and I get a little choked up. Even my familiar can feel how much the path I've chosen is draining on me. He probably just wants me to do what makes me happy. My magic and life force and Momiji's are directly connected. I don't think he feels my feelings, but I know he feels my exhaustion. He knows that charms doesn't come naturally to me, and he likely wants me to practice potions just as much as I do.

I scoop him up and put him over my shoulder, hugging him closely to my chest. Maybe we're both exhausted.

Ping.

I check my phone to see a text from my dad.

> **Dad**
> It was really nice seeing you this past week. Don't be a stranger. Love u.

> **Indigo**
> It was nice to see you too, love you.

However complicated my family can be, it really was nice to see them. Maybe next time my mother will show me more kindness. As it stands, I only visit home for Gratefulness Week. Iris visits during Christmas, Spring Break, random days over the summer. I know, because my mother gloats to me about it, trying to use it to make me feel guilty for not visiting more often. I wish she'd stop to think that maybe I'd visit more if I felt more welcome there—that maybe it's her that keeps me away.

As I start to doze off again, my mind is a maze of emotion. I try to tether myself to reality, that I need to focus on my job, bettering my relationship with my family, and maintaining my friendships, but I am so attached to my dreams. Dreams of working with potions everyday, of coming home to a girlfriend, maybe even one day a wife, and her having green skin. Green skin... and black hair... and a septum piercing... and a tattoo of her favorite constellation. If a shooting star flung itself across the sky right now, that is what I'd wish for.

Beep. Beep. Beep.

What the fuck is that awful sound? Oh right, my alarm.

Beep. Beep. Beep.

My eyes will hardly open as I snooze my alarm for the third time. Wait, third time? Oh shit... it's Monday. I have work today.

INDIGO

I'VE ALWAYS HATED MONDAYS, BUT THIS MONDAY FEELS different. There's a tension in the air, with students buzzing about the school preparing for finals, but there's also a note of excitement. It's subtle–the early Christmas gifts exchanged between friends and the cookies for Hanukkah. Though some of the staff will be here during the break between fall and spring semester, the students will not, so many of them celebrate their holidays early.

Being such a young teacher has its ups and downs. It's annoying to constantly get mistaken for a student– and I believe some mages and staff members take me less seriously–but overall, it's a blessing. I relate to my students on a level many of the other professors won't understand, because I was literally one of them a few years ago in undergrad. And even just last year, I was attending Augury for grad school. Many of the professors here went to other universities around the world. For people like Adeib and Dean Bariel, regardless of where they attended, it was so long ago it might as well have been another lifetime. So here I stand, grateful I'm recognized in our cafeteria. A perk of being a favored professor of the freshmen class is that I get to cut in line.

I'm here because I heard the special dessert of today was cranachan, and it would be an offense to my ancestors if I didn't try some. Composed of cream cheese, oats, raspberries, whip cream, and honey, the Scottish dessert is delectable. I've only had my father's rendition, and he was never the greatest in the kitchen.

My favorite satyr and elf duo, Eden and Raven, let me cut them in the astronomically long line. I usually only see them in my history class, so it's fun to see how they are outside the classroom. They're doing their nails, which amuses me. I never knew there were portable nail kits. I rarely get my nails done, as I've always had too much anxiety about it, scared of all the choices I'd have to make at once. The color, the style. It makes my brain hurt. I turn back around, facing forward.

Emilia, a pink-haired mermaid from one of my charms classes, is in line in front of me. She's not the kind of merfolk that can shift, so she uses a portable tank that runs on magic. The upside of having a tank is that there's room for advertising and decorations. Emilia has decked the backside of her tank with infographics on different political causes she supports, and it amazes me to read them all. Merfolk want their own school, as well as a tubing system so they can swim through Sunspell City without needing a tank. I scan the QR code and sign the petition.

Her phone beeps, and she looks back at me. "Professor Watson? Thank you!"

"Of course," I say, not realizing she'd get an immediate notification.

The line moves quickly, and I get my treat. I snap a

picture, meaning to send it to my Dad, but accidentally press Daelor instead. *Shit.*

> **Vega**
> getting a treat?

> **Indigo**
> Yeah. It's sweet, but not as sweet as you!

I want to punch myself in the face the second I send the text. I hope she doesn't reply, because I don't know what I'd say next.

Crossing towards the Potions Tree, I meet Alitha in the lab. Though I'm not a potions professor, I like to play around with them from time to time, working on personal experiments of my own. Alitha and I have been testing some new concepts. I throw the bamboo cup away and put on a pair of gloves. I would've brought a treat for Alitha, but I don't think they make vegan cranachan.

"How close are you to achieving your desired results?" Alitha asks, watching me rip pieces of fabric and pour the potion onto them.

"I'm close. It works on natural fabrics, but not synthetic blends. I think it needs some sort of honey or honey-like element," I say.

Basic potions are easy. Basic potions that get an object to start or stop doing what it already does are the easy part. Other concepts, like permanent alterations that have nothing to do with the object's intended purpose, are much harder. You can use a simple potion to make a carrot round, or a different color, but you'd need a lot more practice to turn a carrot into a cucumber. This potion has taken me *months*. It is anything but basic.

She hands me a bottle of honey, and I pour a generous amount in, mixing the substances. I pour my new concoction onto the synthetic fabric, and the fibers immediately grow together, fixing the rip I had made.

"We fucking did it," I shout, and Alitha gestures for me to quiet down with her hand. She grabs me into a tight hug, holding me against her tall, lean form and I wrap my arms around her.

"*You* did it," she says.

Tuesday and Wednesday go by in a blur of review packets, study halls, and office hours. Despite how busy I am, all I can think about is this weekend.

A few of my students sneak me little gifts and treats. I think, for some of them, they just want to be nice... for others, this is very clearly a bribe that won't help them on their finals.

Just a few more days until my final date with Vega, I think to myself on the drive home. *Just a few more days until it ends.*

With finals happening tomorrow, today we're having a little study party in my History 101 class. All of my students pitched in. Raven and Eden brought punch and chips. Kwon, a masculine cambion, made a holiday-winter playlist with songs like All I Want For Christmas Is You, Frosty the Snowman, Feliz Navidad, and A Moonflower Solstice. Everyone wants to study in different ways. Many brought textbooks, flashcards, and even tablets.

"What if I put on a game? It'll quiz you about our history, and whoever wins will get ten points of extra credit," I say.

"Yes," shouts two of my students at once. I look over to see Wren, an androgynous-looking cambion, and Zinnia, a feminine satyr, jump out of their seats.

Wren and Zinnia are polar opposites. Wren is thin with red skin and long straight white hair and seems to prefer darkness. From their fluffy sweater, to their miniskirt and lace-up combat boots, everything is pitch black. Even the curved horns on the top of their head are onyx. Zinnia, on the other hand, is like a cloud. Her skin is a light tan, her hair a sage green, and her clothes pastel pink. She's much more curvaceous, with softer lines to her figure. Somehow, through all their opposition, I always see them together, even outside my classroom.

"Get out your devices then," I say with a smile.

Frantically, Wren and Zinnia get out their phones and swiftly join the game while the other students type their names at a normal page. Zinnia taps her foot, impatient as we wait for everyone to get logged in. It's loud—too loud—but I don't say anything. She's just really competitive.

"Could you please quit tapping? It's vexatious at best," Wren says to Zinnia, who crosses her arms.

"Buttercup, I do what I want–and I want to win," Zinnia has a soft, southern accent as speaks. Her voice is somehow sweet yet... there's a sinister note to it. Why is she making such a big deal out of this game?

"What is their deal?" I ask a few students sitting in row behind them.

"I don't know, but they're like this in *every* class," a serpentine, whose name I *think* is Alya, says. Another student rolls his eyes, clearly annoyed at the two. I would find it annoying if it wasn't so entertaining. It's like watching two cats fight.

"Wren, Zinnia, you know this is just for fun, right?" I ask.

"It is most certainly not," Wren says. "You offered ten points extra credit to the winner. If I'm going to be number one and beat Zinnia, I need those points."

Oh gosh... should I have offered candy instead?

The game begins and everyone seems to be having fun—everyone but Zinnia and Wren, who have furious looks on their faces as they type away. They keep trading first and second place, and I have no idea who will come out on top. They're equally brilliant.

Anxiety fills me as I consider what could happen next. What if one of them wins and it causes the other one to have a meltdown... couldn't that be bad for their finals? I can prevent this. I sneak Dahlia a text as I watch what might as well be an olympic-level competition. The entire class is half-assing their answers, solely focused on Zinnia and Wren.

> **Indigo**
> Hey, if I send you an answer key, can you sign up for this game? It's on qahoot.earth, code is 14157.

> **Dahlia**
> Heyyyy Watson. Yeah I can do that but like why?

> **Indigo**
> Long story. Trying to prevent a meltdown in one of my classes. Answer key is: CCDABCDDBAA.

> **Dahlia**
> Gotcha, on it.

Someone with the username HumanGirlyy joins the game, and I know it's Dahlia. Quickly, she pushes Wren into second place and Zinnia into third, claiming first by the end.

"Who is human girly?" Zinnia says with a kind of rage I didn't know was possible. Her vibrant eyes are now violent.

Wren crosses their arms. "I would have won anyway, so just sit down."

"Anyone want to claim human girly?" I ask the class, but everyone shakes their head no. Perfect, just as I had hoped. "It must've been a bot. Sorry, Wren, maybe if you have me next semester."

"I'm a charms minor, so I think I'll have you for one class," they say, running their fingers through their long white strands.

"What did you say?" Zinnia says, and their rivalry is starting to make sense. I don't think either of them have any other friends, so maybe this is the way they developed a friendship—through competition.

"I'm a charms minor?"

"No, I'm a charms minor," Zinnia says, as if only one of those can be the truth.

"It's not mutually exclusive," I say. "You can both get a minor in charms."

"Okay, but we can't both be number one," Wren says with fervor. "That *is* mutually exclusive."

An elfborn human stands and walks over to the speaker, turning the music up so loud that I can no longer hear Wren and Zinnia argue. I'm going to miss this group of freshmen, just maybe not all the arguing.

On the drive home Friday afternoon, Momiji curls up in the passenger seat, snoozing away. My students all did fantastic on their finals; I only had to fail one girl, but she skipped nearly every class... that's not my fault.

I'm excited for the much needed break from classes, from responsibility. Unfortunately, Dr. Lothiel requested I plan our legendary Augury University Christmas Party. It's not technically a Christmas party, as we encompass many holidays, but it might as well be with the amount of Christmas lights and spiked eggnog there is every year, as told to me by Alitha.

I'm the one running it; I want it to be next level epic, but I'm also afraid. What if it sucks and someone else gets to do it next year? Or what if I'm so amazing at planning it becomes my new responsibility?

I decide to turn off that part of my brain to the best of my abilities and just listen to the soft violin playing through my radio. Tomorrow is my date with Vega, and I'm going to allow myself to enjoy it. I deserve this, and so does she. *Just one last time*, I tell myself. I'm not sure I'm very convincing.

fifteen
INDIGO

It's finally Saturday. Having spent the entire week trying to ignore how quickly this day was coming up, nervous energy still tumbles around in my belly. Vega had texted me telling me to dress for the cold, so dress for the cold I do.

Pulling my tight black pants up my legs, I pick out a purple long sleeve top to go with it and put it on over my head, tucking the bottom into the pants. I decide to keep my makeup light, topped with a glossy black lipstick. The final touch to complete the look? A long scarf. I yank on my boots and tuck a pair of gloves into my purse, alongside all the other goodies I have stuffed in there. Emergency potions, chapstick, mints—you name it.

Ring.

The doorbell. Already? I open the door to find exactly what I expected. Vega. She's wearing tight black pants as well with a form-fitting jacket in a fuschia color. We practically match, and I giggle with excitement. Blowing a kiss towards Momiji, I shut the door.

"Where to?" I ask. I want to know what we're doing so bad, but she insisted it be a surprise.

"Boca Raton," she informs me. "But first, this." V gets out a black piece of fabric and moves behind me, wrapping the fabric around my head, blindfolding me. I feel my face flush as she takes me by the hand and escorts me to her car.

It feels like we've been driving forever. I know it's only been an hour or so, but without knowing where we are, time moves strangely. There's Christmas music playing over the radio, and I listen as Vega quietly sings along. She's actually kind of good, which only adds to my long list of reasons I find her attractive.

V's hand rests on my leg, and I suddenly wish I had worn shorts so I could feel the warmth of her skin against mine. Her cologne—perfume—whatever it is… it's woodsy, with hints of cinnamon and peppermint, and it goes with the energy of the day. It's really December.

The car comes to a stop, and I move to remove my blindfold when Vega stops me. "Not yet," she says. "First, we've got to walk for a few minutes."

She gets out of the car and opens my door, taking me by the hand, leading me to who knows where. There's Christmas music playing, and I can hear the bustle of a crowd in the near distance.

"Vega, can I take this thing off now?"

"Yes."

Untying the blindfold, I look up to see Vega smiling down at me, but when she moves, my mouth opens in awe. There's a colossal fucking snow globe behind her. A small-theme-park-sized snow globe. *Holy shit.*

"How? What is this?" I ask, shock still lingering on my face.

"It's called Winter Wonderland. A bunch of illusionary mages got together and designed a theme park that feels like you're inside a snow globe. Let's go inside," she says, interlocking our fingers and leading me to the entrance.

There's a door on one side of the base, and a cambion dressed as one of Santa's helpers takes our ticket stubs. Entering the park, it's ethereal. Bright white and pastel Christmas lights are everywhere. A tiny snowflake falls onto my shoulder, and I turn to Vega, the corners of my mouth ticking upward.

"There's snow?"

She grins wide. "That was the big reason I wanted to bring you here. I know it's not real snow, but—"

"It's perfect," I interrupt. "Just perfect. I've never seen snow, real or fake, so it doesn't make a difference to me." This is one of the sweetest gestures anyone has ever made towards me, and I could just about cry if I weren't filled with so much joy.

I've never really gone out with anyone who showed me this much kindness. Terranova and I never dated, as he caught feelings for my sister instead of me. Thomas, my only long term partner, broke up with me after being accepted to a trade school in The Americas. There was Amber. And Walnut. And Mai. But those were all short college flings. Sexy and meaningless. This is the first connection I've felt in years, and however fleeting it might be, it's real.

"Have you ever been ice skating?" Vega asks, and I scrunch my nose.

"I've been a few times, but just at one of those skating rinks in a mall, nothing fancy."

We cross towards the rink, which is interesting. It's as if a frozen lake and a skating rink had a baby. It's outside in the open air, but there's a glass wall with a railing surrounding it. There are couples skating around, and mothers with their children. There's even a faun spinning and performing jumps.

Walking up to the counter, a centaur wearing a bright green polo greets us with a mustache-covered smile. "Greetings, I'm Larry with Winter Wonderland. How can I help you two lovely ladies?"

"We'd like to go skating. Can we rent two pairs?" Vega asks, tone jovial and polite. Her hair is down, but she pushed all of it to one side so it looks like half her head is shaved. I stare at her long, pretty strands.

"What size?"

"Size eleven and size… five?" she says, though she doesn't sound confident.

"Close. I'm a six," I correct her.

"That'll be twelve dabloons."

Vega puts her phone against the reader, and it beeps, accepting her e-payment. The man goes over to the shelf and picks up two pairs of skates, one black and one white, and hands them over to us. Sitting on a nearby bench, we put them on. I wore fluffy white socks, and the tops hang over the skates.

Vega pulls out her gloves, and I do the same, excited to skate with her. I've never been super into ice skating. Iris really enjoyed roller skating; she was on a derby team when we were kids. Me? I tended to prefer things that didn't have high chances of me falling on my ass. Skating with Vega would be different though.

Getting onto the ice, I'm a little wobbly, rocking back and forth to try and not fall. Vega, on the other hand, is smooth as silk, gliding beside me. She takes me by the hand and helps me balance. At first, I'm completely leaning against her, but after a while, we only have to hold hands.

I look into Vega's golden eyes. "Can I make a confession?"

"Always."

"When I was a kid, I was super jealous of the girls who could do skating and dance tricks. I was never talented or flexible enough, and of course I never trained hard enough for it because for so many others it came so naturally."

"I'm sorry, little rabbit. Do you want to try a trick right now?" she asks, and I blanche.

"I don't think that's a good idea."

"Sure it is. Trust me, I'll charm your skates."

Vega pulls me in close and lifts me from my hips. Without any work, my legs lift up and swing back, and it feels like I'm flying beside her. When she puts me down, she keeps control of my skates so that I safely land.

We skate around some more until our legs grow tired, and Vega pulls me over to the sidelines. "Do you want to go get a bite to eat?"

I nod, my stomach growling. "It's a little late to be grabbing lunch, so maybe there won't be a huge line?" I say.

"Huge line or no line, doesn't matter to me. We've got all day."

We get off the ice and trade the skates for our boots.

"I think there's a restaurant on the other side, let's head there," Vega says.

We walk through the park, passing a group of Christmas carolers. There are children taking photos with a man dressed as Santa Claus, and a performer is juggling toys. There are smaller rides, and lots of little stands with snack food.

"Are you sure you don't want to just get something from one of the stands?" I ask.

"No, let's go inside and sit down. There's something I want you to try," she insists, and so I follow.

We get to a building which looks like an actual gingerbread house. The roof is lined with fake icing, and there are people-sized gumdrops sticking out of the top. A hostess wearing a candy cane-esque dress brings us to our table and hands us two menus. As we wait for our waitress, Vega holds the menus, not handing one over, and I look at her funny.

"Can I look at the menu?"

"Nope," she says and winks.

I want to be mad, want to demand she hand it over, but I'm not. It's super sexy when she does stuff like this, and so far, I've never been disappointed with the results.

Our waitress comes over, and she looks like a Christmas tree. Her green dress has light up bulbs that sparkle as she walks. "What can I get you two?"

"We'll have the hot chocolate flight, an order of the Christmas charcuterie board, and a large side of sweet potato fries. Oh, and two waters, please," Vega says with more confidence than I've ever mustered in my life. I have a tendency to stutter and mumble when I order food; anxiety really is a bitch.

"Thank you," I whisper as the waitress takes our menu and walks away.

When she returns, she's got a tray with two waters and a piece of wood covered with mugs full of hot chocolate. Prior to today, I'd only heard of flights of beer and liquor. She places everything on the table, and I notice each mug has a label in front of it. Peppermint. Dark Chocolate Raspberry. Caramel. Cinnamon. S'mores. It all sounds so good.

"Which one do you want to try first?"

"Hmm. I'm not a big fan of caramel. The rest all sound so good, you pick," I say.

Vega picks up a spoon and dips it into the whip cream, then the cinnamon hot chocolate. She places one hand under my chin, and I open my mouth, allowing her to place it on my tongue. The richness of the cinnamon mixed with the chocolate is delectable, and I can't help but make a little sound of appreciation.

"I usually hear that sound in a different context," V says, and I snort. I touch my nose, shocked that hot chocolate isn't coming out of it.

We take turns feeding spoons full of hot chocolate to one another, and I'm incredibly grateful to be in this moment. Partially because of how wonderful this moment is, but also partially because we must look incredibly cringey and love-stricken in this moment, draped over the table, romantically sharing a flight of hot chocolate. This is like something out of one of those bad Christmas romance movies my sister would watch every year. I love it. I'm the main fucking character—I might as well move to an abandoned farm and try to revive it by selling Christmas trees with the help of the town's mysterious sexy lesbian lumberjack, Dr. Vega Daelor.

When our food arrives, everything is perfect. One half of the charcuterie board is meats, crackers, and cheeses. The other half is pumpkin bars, sugar cookies, and peppermint bark. Vega stuffs her face with meat and cheese, while I wholly consume the sweet potato fries. The vibes here are immaculate, and I feel like I'm in Christmas heaven.

After we finish eating and pay, Vega takes me outside. The snow is falling harder now, and there's a big field with piles of it to the left of us.

"Can we build a snowman?" I ask, and the childlike grin that spreads across her face is priceless.

"Of course we fucking can."

sixteen

VEGA

I BEGIN WORKING ON THE BODY OF THE SNOWMAN, WHILE Indigo collects sticks and rocks to form its arms and legs. We should've saved a sweet potato fry for his nose, but we'll figure something out. As we work on our masterpiece, Indigo seems to take notice with a couple walking by.

"Shit. Uh—Vega—I... that's Malik," Indigo whispers.

"Malik Hills, as in our coworker?" I ask.

"Yes, let's go." She grabs me by the sleeve of my jacket, dragging me towards some bushes.

My pants get caught on a branch, and as she pulls me forward, they rip. It's nothing crazy, but I can feel the chill air on my thigh now. We huddle on the ground behind a bush as Malik and his girlfriend walk by. I didn't even know he had a girlfriend. She's cute—clearly a faunborn—and they pass us quickly, holding hands and kissing one another.

"I ripped my pants," I say, showing her the tear in the fabric. She opens her purse and digs out a small vial.

"I don't know why, but I just knew this would come

in handy," she says as she pours some of the liquid onto my pants, the fibers instantly growing back into themselves.

"You're fucking with me," I say aloud. Where did she get that? Magical potions can't be mass produced because nobody has enough magic to do so. If you have a magic potion, it's either because you made it yourself, or you were gifted it from someone else. "Did Alitha give that to you?"

"No actually," Indigo starts. "I made it. It's one of the main projects I've been working on."

"That's amazing," I say, grabbing her head between my hands and kissing her on the forehead. "You're amazing, Indigo."

"Thank you. Also, I think we're safe to get up now," she says, and I help her stand. "What's the next plan, Dr. Daelor?"

I almost blush every time she calls me that. She's the only one that has that effect on me. "Well, we're going to watch a movie on the lawn, but that's not for a couple more hours...."

"And?"

I clear my throat. I'm not nervous, it's more like excitement bubbling within me. "I heard there's a part of the park that's closed off for construction."

"Closed off like... nobody will be over there?" Indigo's cheeks flush.

"Precisely, little rabbit," I whisper. "Because the noises you make should be for me and me alone."

We move towards the back of the park where they're working on a small theater, as well a mini-Christmas village. Passing through the small cottages that presumably belong to Santa's helpers, I dip my head as we enter one that looks more complete. Once we're both inside, I realize there's nothing here except a few tools on the floor and a little portable heater. Perfect.

I shrug off my jacket, placing it on the floor. Indigo looks up at me with those big violet eyes, and I can barely help myself. Shoving her against the wall, my head ducked down into the crook of her neck, I kiss her soft skin as I use my knee to create friction, right where she likes it.

"Vega," she moans out as I suck on her throat.

Indigo takes one finger and pushes it underneath my jaw, bringing me into a kiss. Our tongues collide, and I keep rubbing my knee, doing my best to make sure I'm hitting her clit through her pants. She whimpers, kissing me harder before going silent. She shudders with release and pushes me back with an undeniable force that I've never seen from her. "Oh, what is this? Do you think you're in control?" I ask, licking my teeth and tusks.

Indigo wraps her leg around me and kicks the back of my leg, toppling us down to the ground. Now on top of me, she grins as hard as she's blushing. "No, but I can sure try. Let me give you what you want." Her voice is like a plea—like a song, and I give in. I'd give her anything she asked for, even my heart.

She wriggles my pants completely off, and I shimmy out of my longsleeve shirt. Pulling off my boxer briefs, Indigo takes in a deep breath before crawling up between my legs, and I rest my back onto the hard ground.

The slow, soft drag of her tongue is simultaneously everything I need, and nowhere close to enough. My leg twitches as she swirls her tongue, dancing it around my clit. My back arches as she digs her fingers into my thighs, further pushing my legs apart.

I love looking down and watching her between my legs. My thighs are strong enough to crush her, and yet like a good little rabbit, she stays there. Perfect prey.

"I want your fingers," I say, voice low with desire. She slowly trails them up towards my swollen lips. "Now." Two fingers gently enter my opening, and as I moan out in pleasure, practically whimpering, she drives them deeper inside me. Thrusting her fingers while sucking on my clit, Indigo gives me everything I could have ever asked for.

But when has she not?

Toppling over the edge, my body twitches as I let out a long, staccato breath.

"Good gir—"

"Don't," I interrupt. "Or I'll stick a vibrator in your panties and control it while we walk around."

"You'd have to have one with you," she teases.

"Who says I don't?"

Once my skin is no longer slick with sweat, we put our clothes back on and exit the construction zone, careful not to be caught as we sneak out the doors, back into the main part of the park. There's a little stand selling popcorn, and I send the man five dabloons for a bucket. The sun is setting in a cotton candy sky, and our fingers intertwine as we make our way to the field. There's a big screen with a projector, and we sit down as the opening scene of Elf comes on.

"Honestly, the main actor looks more like an elf than

all of those tiny people. Elves are usually tall," Indigo whispers to where only I can hear.

"Yeah, but the smaller elves remind me more of you," I whisper against her ear. Sometimes Indigo explains elves to me like they aren't the majority of the population of the Isles of Magia. Although it's usually stuff I know, it's still cute to see her so interested in her magical origins. Perhaps I should get to know the human part of me too.

Her eyebrows scrunch, and she frowns for a second before giving out a small giggle. Snuggling up to Indigo, we watch the movie with my arms wrapped around her.

I don't play music on the drive back to Sunspell City. Indigo is curled up in the passenger seat, snoring away. This isn't the last time I'll see her–hell, she's my subordinate; I can see her everyday if I want to, but this is the last time I'll get to be with her.

I have to be the one to end this. She doesn't have the strength to do it. I know that we both value our jobs, I know that we both have feelings for one another, but I think it's too much for her. If I told her to drop it all and go with me to live in The Americas or—or even off-world on fucking Barac, she'd probably go. She wants someone to make that decision for her, but I can't let her.

Indigo allowed someone to control her for her entire life. Her mother was the puppet master, pulling her strings. Indigo went to Augury University and cut those strings, but now she's desperate to hand them over to someone new. I won't let it be me, and I sure as hell won't let it be her mother again.

We stop at a light, and I take a mental snapshot of her cute little body, all huddled up against me as she sleeps somberly. I make note of the sound of her voice. Her laugh. And the look she gives me when she smiles—when she comes. I try to record it all, tuck it into my heart for later. She may not get to be mine in this lifetime, but maybe in another.

Once we're in the city, I drive really slow. I could get ticketed for going this far under the speed limit, but I don't fucking care anymore. All I want is more time, something I'd never valued much until recently. Pulling into her driveway, I stop the car. I don't wake her up... No, not yet. I just brush my finger against the soft skin of her cheek and try not to let out the tear threatening to fall.

Am I really getting teary-eyed over a goodbye with someone I'll see in a few weeks? Man. This screams abandonment issues, doesn't it? A big screw you to anyone who has ever called me a player. Clearly I'm not very good at playing.

I lightly brush Indigo's shoulder, and she makes an eyes-half-closed hand gesture for me to carry her. Getting out of the car, I go over to the passenger's side and scoop her up into my arms.

After entering the house and removing our boots and coats, I lay her down onto her bed, before kissing her cheek and crossing to the door.

"Vega, will you stay with me?" she whispers, voice weak.

I don't know how to say no to her.

Crawling into bed, I snuggle up behind her, basking

in her natural scent. Before I know it, she's snoring, and I drift alongside her.

Indigo stirs, barely awake as I give her one last kiss goodbye; her lips are as soft as clouds. I walk over to the door and wave at Momiji, who makes a whimpering noise.

"I know you'll miss Freja, but you can see her at school," I say.

The white little rabbit frowns. Little rabbit—that was Indigo's nickname before I ever knew about her familiar. It truly is like we were meant to be, at least one day. I just wish that day was today.

seventeen
INDIGO

I wake to an empty bed. No warm, green, muscled body sleeping next to me. Just a cold, lonely gap where Vega was. I worried she was going to leave in the middle of the night. I actually didn't expect her to stay, but she did. I need coffee. Walking into the kitchen, I find Momiji moping on the dining room table, staring down at a scrap of paper.

She left a note?

indie,
i care about you so much that i have to say goodbye.
be kind to yourself. i am so glad i got to experience this with you, however short it was.
thank you. i'll see you around.
-v

It's really over. I mean, it had never truly begun... we

always knew this wasn't allowed, that it wouldn't work, but we gave into our whims and desires. She is an obsession. A fixation. I should be able to move on soon, I just need a little time.

What if nobody ever wants me like that? Or what if nobody ever makes me feel that good again? I shake my head, pushing away those thoughts, and wipe the tears that are falling down my face.

It's been a week since I've seen Vega. An entire week without her sultry smile, a week without the deep notes in her voice. Without work to distract me, I've been an anxious mess. I decide to text the Unholy Trilogy.

> **Indigo**
> I am fucking sad, friends.

They both reply instantly.

> **Alitha**
> We know.

> **Dahlia**
> What did you do all day?

> **Indigo**
> ...

> **Dahlia**
> Watsonnnn

> **Indigo**
> I cried into a bucket of ice cream.

The next thing I know, I've got an incoming call from Torres.

"Hello?" I pick up.

"Indigo, Alitha, can you hear me?" Dahlia asks.

"I can hear you," Alitha replies.

"I'm here. I can hear you."

"Perfect." Dahlia pauses to take in a deep breath. "This is broken-off-engagement level relationship mourning for a holiday fling. I know you fell hard, but it's get your shit together time, Watson."

As harsh as it is, she's right.

"Why don't we all go out together tomorrow night?" Alitha suggests. "I've got news to share, anyhow. What about that one bar—"

"Not the best idea. That's where they met. Why don't we go to dinner; how's Italian food sound?"

"Perfect," I reply. Besides grocery shopping and long walks with Momiji, I've barely left the house. "Tomorrow at six?"

"Great," Alitha says.

Dahlia makes kissing sounds into the phone before hanging up.

Plans. Alright, now I have plans. At least that'll give me something new to spiral about instead of my forbidden relationship.

I pull up to the restaurant in a sweater dress and tights. They're the kind that look transparent but actually have a fleece lining on the inside. I wonder if they make them in green or red. I've seen them from the fairest white to the deepest brown, but I'm not sure I've seen them for non-human, non-elf skin tones. I wonder if Vega has ever gone to buy a pair.

Dahlia is in an off-the-shoulder, sexy sweater dress with heels, and Alitha in a long white dress that hugs her tightly, with knee-high boots to match.

The three of us walk into the Italian restaurant and every head turns. I know my friends are gorgeous, but damn, even I feel good tonight. The hostess seats us at a booth in the corner; Alitha and Dahlia slide in across from me.

"Okay history person, why do we call it Italian food?" Dahlia asks.

"There's a region in Europa called Italia, named after the country Italy that used to be there. Countries may have disbanded their governments after The Convergence, but most of the cultures are still alive," I explain.

"Oh, so it's like how my mom says we're Puerto Rican and Portuguese, even though those aren't countries anymore, but more so regions within their continents?" Dahlia asks.

"Yeah!" I confirm.

"I guess I'm just confused on why us humans are so obsessed with the past. I feel like most of the magical races don't give a shit about what happened prior to The Convergence," Dahlia says.

The waiter interrupts us to take our orders. Dahlia orders herself and I margaritas. Alitha orders a glass of white wine.

"I think the majority of people without any human blood don't care because Earth prior to The Convergence really has nothing to do with them," I say. "Whereas we're tied to the past through culture, blood, and history."

"See, I try to learn about both Earth's history, as well as Loria," Alitha chimes in.

I smile. "I try to learn everything. I'm like a sponge."

Dahlia grabs a piece of bread and dips it into the olive oil and spices. "Enough about history. Alitha, what's your big news?"

"Laurel Gilbert, Chair of the Potions Department, is leaving Augury University," she says, blue-eyes wide. "And they offered me the position." Alitha's hand moves to cover her mouth. Her nails are white with little blue snowflakes, and they contrast beautifully to the deep brown of her skin.

My jaw practically unhinges itself as I finally process what she just shared. There's a new availability in the Potions Department. Holy shit.

Dahlia looks at us with eyebrows raised. "I was going to say congrats, but you both look concerned. This is a good thing, right? You'll be making way more money."

"And I'll have a lot more responsibility," Alitha shares. "But this also means I'll need to hire my replacement."

A grin spreads across Dahlia's gorgeous face. "You could hire Indigo. That's like her dream!"

Alitha's mouth forms a thin line. "I can't just hire my best friend, there's a whole process involved, and they'd likely accuse me of nepotism."

"Okay, fine. But you should still apply," Dahlia says, looking at me.

"I'll think about it."

We all order pasta and stuff our faces with bread as we wait for our meals to come out. Alitha recommends her new nail tech, and I write the name down, though I'm still unsure I'll ever get the courage to go get mine done. Maybe if someone went with me.

"I have a new client," Dahlia says, her voice full of mystery.

I place my fork on my plate and put my elbows up on the table and rest my head in my hands. "Tell us more."

"She's an elf. Her hair is like twelve feet long, but she usually wears it in a bun," Dahlia shares. "It took me two days to give her highlights and trim the dead ends. I charged her a few thousand dabloons."

"That's intense," Alitha says.

"Yeah. She wouldn't stop talking about history, which I think is why my brain keeps thinking about it."

"Wait," I say. "What was her name?"

"Elia? Elara?"

"That's Dr. Lothiel, one of my bosses," I say with a laugh, trying not to think of my other boss. "Her hair is twelve feet long?"

"Something like that. How did you not know?"

"She's never worn it down," Alitha shares. "Ever. It's always in a bun. We knew it was long, but not that long." She takes another bite of her cheeseless pasta.

"Honestly, I kind of just assumed her hair was really thick, that's so funny." I crinkle my nose. "I wonder if she'll wear it down now that it's all fancy."

"We'll see at the Christmas party," Alitha says.

Sitting at my desk in my little house, I hover my mouse over the submit button on my application. I had gotten an email from Augury University suggesting anyone can apply, but that they'll be looking at applicants from outside the organization as well. I know what's going to happen. I'm going to get my hopes up, they'll hire some potions professor with years of experience from somewhere else, and they'll probably even give them relocation assistance.

Why would they hire me? I'm an adjunct with no formal potions training. I majored in charms and minored in history, much to my own dismay. If I could go back in time, I would. I'd be a potions professor working alongside Alitha, and I'd be dating Vega. Everything in my life would be perfect.

But it's not. So here I am, paloma in hand, crying and drinking my feelings. Simone told me I have to stop using sugar and alcohol to make me feel better, and although I agree, I can't heed that advice tonight. I've been thinking about this for days—ever since Alitha told me. Dahlia has been hounding me to put in my application before it's too late, so screw it. Here goes nothing.

Click.

I want to feel relieved, but all I feel is nervous. What if they interview me? What if I'm actually given a chance, will I fuck it up?

The Christmas party is just a week away. I load up my car with all the projects I've been working on. I've got fake present boxes, strings of snowflakes, and even giant paper poinsettias. Iris would always find new hobbies she wanted to try; every year it was something new. One year, it was arts-and-crafts, and she decided she wanted me to try it with her. We made a whole scene, a room of decorations. There were houses and flowers and all sorts of things. I don't know if she does arts-and-crafts anymore, but it's something I'll always be fond of.

Getting into the car, Momiji in tow, I head towards the Illusionary Jungle. This is going to be a party to remember.

eighteen
VEGA

I do laundry once a week. From my bedsheets to my winter jackets, I wash everything. I think it's one of the things she liked about me—she liked how clean my apartment was.

The first week, I could still smell the remnants of her. It was faint, barely there, but my orc nose allowed me to notice.

The second week, it was barely a note. Maybe I once had my arms around a woman, and this was that smell– but maybe not.

Now, the scent is gone entirely. As is the sound of her laugh, and the look in her eyes. It's pathetic how much I miss her. She wasn't a craving I could manage; she was my every desire wrapped up in a neat little bow, just in time for Jul and Christmas.

After I left Indigo's house, I spent an hour sifting through our employment contracts for the third time, just to be sure. Nope. Still not allowed, not unless one of us switched departments.

I spent the following few weeks working out,

drinking protein shakes, and meditating. I ignored the lack of texts from my father, ignored work emails, and ignored Freja's whining for me to practice my magic.

I gave myself time to mourn and mope, but now I've got to pull myself back up onto my feet and be the strong independent orc that I am. Opening my laptop, I check my emails.

Spam. Spam. Last minute holiday sales. More spam.

An open position. This email is from the dean.

Once I finish reading the email in its entirety, I jump out of my chair, throw on a vest and a pair of pants, and haul ass towards my car. Freja follows, trying to keep up with me.

"Freja, I've fucking figured it out. I know exactly what I need to do so that Indigo and I can be together." I just hope it's not too late. He sent that email days ago.

I drove so fast that even with my windows rolled up, my hair likely looks tousled, but I don't care.

Augury University is a massive campus. Besides the six large camphor trees, there's also fields, fallen logs, and courtyards galore. I sprint my way to the History Tree, climbing up a series of stairs and ladders. Freja flies next to me, taking breaks to sit on my shoulder. I could've waited to be escorted up, but I don't have the time for that. Finding Dean Bariel's office building, a decent sized hut that sticks out of the side of the History Tree, all the way at the top. I can see him speaking to someone through the three glass window panes, and I cross my arms. I can wait. Being rude won't help Indigo's chances.

The elf woman leaves, and I calmly knock on the door, trying not to seem frantic. The Dean opens the door.

"Dr. Daelor, come in." He's tall, though not as tall as me. His body is extremely lanky, and his features are angular, bird-like.

"How has your winter vacation been so far?" I ask in an attempt to make small talk.

"It's been quite nice. Winter Solstice is only a few days away, as you probably know."

"I hope it's everything you wish for," I say. He gestures for me to sit down, and he sits behind his desk, which is a hurricane of paperwork. Freja nuzzles herself against his hand, and he gently pets the top of her colorful little head.

"Thank you. What brings you this way?"

"It's about the job opening—"

"Oh?" His forehead creases, ocean blue eyes squinting at me.

"I think you should pick Indigo—I mean, Professor Watson."

He crosses his arms. "Your charms adjunct? She's an applicant, and I was considering interviewing her."

"Choose her. She's an amazing mage, sir. You will not regret it."

"If she's so amazing, why do you want her out of your department?"

I clear my throat. "She's... she's better at potions. She's not a bad charms mage, that's not what I'm saying, but I've seen her do potions. She created one that fixed a hole in my pants, she's got another one that can help women sense danger; she's truly something."

"So why did she specialize in charms?"

"Familial pressure. It's been great having her in my

department, and she works well with Professor Hills and I, but I think she would be better suited replacing Dr. Taylor," I say, and it is brutal honesty. She has been great, not a single student complained about her... but potions is where she belongs. It's what brings her joy, and it'll allow her to be with me. A fucking win-win if I've ever heard one.

"Can I see some of her potions? I'd like to witness this mastery myself," he says, and I scratch the back of my neck.

"I'm not sure where she keeps them, but Dr. Taylor could probably tell you."

"I'll check with Alitha. I make no promises, but I will heavily consider Professor Watson. Thank you for your recommendation. It's been a pleasure having you join our team."

We shake hands, and Freja hops onto my shoulder. Exiting, I step out and make my way down the History Tree. I stop in my tracks when I smell Indigo.

Standing on a ladder on one of the platforms, Indigo is hanging string lights all around. Dressed in her usual-all black, she's got billowing sleeves and tall chunky boots on. Not ideal for what she's doing, but she looks damn good doing it. I cross towards her, even though I know I shouldn't.

As I get closer, I realize she's accidentally wrapped herself in the lights.

"Indie, are you okay?" I ask.

She yelps, falling off the ladder, and I dart towards her. Catching her in my arms, Indigo looks down at me with her bright violet eyes. I hold her for just a moment, not wanting to let her go.

"Hi," she says, before wiggling. "You can put me down."

"I know—"

"Vega," she says sternly.

Placing her down onto the platform, I help her untangle herself from the lights. "Doing some decorating?"

"Yeah! The Christmas party is Friday," she says. "You would know if you ever checked your email."

"How do you know I don't check my email?"

"Because I know you," she says, and there's a small sprinkle of sadness in her tone. "And because you never RSVP'd."

"Well, I'll be there." I back away from Indigo, and Freja lets out a little squeak.

"Momiji is at home, baby, but you can see him at the party," she says and then looks me straight in the eyes. "I'll see you there."

I turn. Unlike the ancient myth of Orpheus and Eurydice, I don't look back.

Two days until the Christmas party. I sift through my sweater drawer, looking for anything to wear when I see Indigo.

Knock knock.

Someone's at my door?

Knock knock knock.

Someone impatient is at my door. Willing my legs to carry me faster than I have before, I sprint to the front of my apartment, opening the door. Indigo launches herself at me, grabbing my face and kissing me harshly. Her face is wet with tears, and I wrap myself around her pulling her onto the couch with me.

"My little rabbit, why are you here? Why did you kiss me?"

She wipes away a tear and looks at me with the biggest smile. "I got the job. I'm not your subordinate anymore; we can be together."

"Really?" *This isn't a dream?* I cup her face in my hands.

"Oh, don't act like you didn't know. The Dean said you practically begged him to kick me out of your department." She crosses her arms.

"I did *not*. I specifically said you were amazing, but that you'd be better suited as a potions professor," I say. "Also, I didn't know. I simply made a recommendation. I wasn't sure it would work."

"V, this is all I've ever wanted."

"Wow, I'm flattered."

She pushes me lightly. "Not just you, asshole. All of it. This is everything I've ever dreamed of—everything my mother told me I couldn't have."

"But you can have it," I tell her.

"Because of you."

I shake my head. "No Indigo, you did this. You're the one who graduated early and got a job at Augury University at the age of twenty four. You're the one who took a chance with me at that bar—the one who manages to teach charms and history and practice potion. You're the one who has done all this work, allow yourself to take credit for it. You deserve this."

She kisses me again, this time deeper, and I allow her to take control. "Do I get a reward?"

"Of course," I slowly drift my fingers up her thigh.

"Have I made the naughty or nice list?" she asks, voice full of sin.

"Obviously naughty." I move to unbutton her pants. "What do you want Santa to bring you this year?" I ask with a wink.

"A girlfriend."

My heart grows ten times in size. "I think I can arrange that."

"Wake up sleepy orc," Indigo says, and I roll over.

"Sleep."

"I've got to get going."

At that, my eyes shoot open. "Going where? It's like eight in the morning."

Indigo, already dressed and ready to go, stands over me. "I've got to set up for the party tonight. I'll see you there."

"Are we not going together?" I ask, holding her hand so she can't go yet.

"I don't think it's the best idea to hard launch our relationship at the annual holiday party."

"Fine. We'll drive separately, but I'm spending the entire night by your side."

"Deal," she says and kisses me on the cheek.

I should probably wrap her gifts. She wanted a girlfriend for Christmas, but I already gave her that. A pair of earrings and a strap-on will have to do.

nineteen

INDIGO

EVERYTHING IS PERFECT. ALITHA AND AURA SHOWED UP AROUND three to help me finish setting up. We discussed what classes I'll be taking over from Alitha, and I told Aura about some of the sight students she should expect to meet soon. Augury University truly feels like home to me.

As the clock strikes five, people start to make their way in. The trees are covered in lights, sparkling bright so all can see.

Don't stress, I remind myself. *It's going to be awesome.*

To get into the meeting room, guests have to enter through an archway covered in fake Christmas presents. There are shimmery snowflakes dangling from the ceiling, and a gorgeous tree in one corner for everyone to place their gifts under. Dr. Ali and Dr. McNab are the first to arrive. Adeib brought tabbouleh, and Feather brought a large vat of mac-n-cheese. Others trail in not long after, carrying their gifts and treats. There's white chocolate lemon truffles, lasagne, and more. Our librarian, Chak Rokismith, brought a whole turkey.

"You did a fantastic job, Professor Watson," Dr.

Lothial says, hovering over me. "I couldn't be more impressed. I mean the poinsettia photo wall? This whole thing is effortlessly charming."

"Thank you. It definitely took a lot of effort," I reply.

Vega is almost the last to arrive, walking in with a decent-sized box covered in purple wrapping paper and a grocery bag. I'm honestly surprised she read the email far enough to know we're playing Dirty Santa.

She comes up to me in her green, chunky knit sweater, and quickly kisses my forehead. Freja flies in after her, practically crashing into Momiji before the two make their way to the charcuterie board to steal cheese and crackers.

"I brought this as a treat," Vega says, and I open the paper bag, which includes a box of hot chocolate packets and a bag of marshmallows. Very Vega.

After all the food is on the table and all the gifts are under the tree, we start a line and get to eating. I make sure to get a scoop of everything, and Vega gets two.

Seated between Vega and Alitha, munching on some delicious food, I watch the dean stand and raise his glass. "I wanted to make a toast for Professor Watson. Though she may not be a charms professor anymore, she sure knows how to throw a charming party. I cannot wait to see what you and Dr. Taylor do with the Potions Department"

Everyone raises their glasses, and I could cry—I could, but I've cried enough in the last few weeks. A grin spreads across my face, as well as a flush of pink.

Transforming into an owl, he flies around the room before landing on our table, winking, and shifting back.

"Did he just wink at me in owl form?" I ask the table. I didn't know owls *could* wink.

"I don't know, but I don't believe I've had enough spiked eggnog," Aura says.

"I remember seeing an owl at a previous meeting, but I didn't put two and two together," Malik says. "Archeron is a bird?"

"Dean Bariel is an elf with the rare ability to shift forms," Alitha explains. "Your eyes did not deceive you."

"Everyone, move your chairs into a circle," I say, and they all follow along. Furniture is being shifted around left and right until we make a circle in the center of the room.

Though not all our staff is here, there's a good group of ten of us. Vega, Alitha, Malik, Aura, Adeib, Feather, Dr. Lothial, Chak, Dean Bariel, and myself. Each one brought a different, uniquely wrapped gift.

Vega's golden eyes are wide as she looks over towards the pile in the center. "Indigo," she whispers in my ear. "What is going on?"

"Dirty Santa," I explain. "Didn't you read the email?"

"I did not."

"Oh, well. What was the gift for?"

"For you," she says, her tone stern. I don't know what she's so riled up about, but she's got to let loose.

I shrug. "Guess you'll have to win it back."

She goes to say something else, but I shoo her away, ready to start the game. "Alright everyone. Is anyone confused about the rules for Dirty Santa?"

"Same rules as White Elephant?" Chak asks.

"Same rules." I nod, and he gives me a thumbs up. When nobody else says anything, I continue. "Alright. Alitha, how about you open the first gift?"

Alitha walks over and grabs a small blue box, the one Aura had brought.

"Go ahead and open it," I say.

Alitha unwraps the gift to reveal a small golden ornament. It's Augury University, or at least the six camphor trees.

"Wow, someone outdid themselves," I say.

One by one, everyone goes about selecting and opening gifts. There's a small violin that plays music, a mini waffle maker, and other fun items.

As each person makes their selection, Vega's leg shakes faster and faster, the stress emanating off of her.

"Are you okay?" I ask.

"Not in the slightest," she confesses. I'm really worried about her. Maybe the gift she got me was expensive, and she's worried she won't have anything to give me now? I mean, that's silly, but I chose myself to go last for a reason. I'll just steal it from whoever opens it.

Dean Bariel does a little dance as he shimmies his way over to the pile and grabs the purple box that Vega had brought. Sitting down, he slowly starts to unwrap the gift.

"Wait," Vega shouts, standing up. This is so unlike her. "I'm afraid I might have accidentally switched that gift with a different one; can I open it privately first?"

"Absolutely not, that would ruin all the fun," Dean Bariel teases. God, he's insufferable. He continues to slowly take off the wrapping, purposefully taking his time to torture Vega.

"It's nothing bad," Aura says to Vega, but the tension doesn't leave her body until he opens the box to reveal a much smaller velvet box.

"Another box. This better not be the gift, Vega."

"Open it," I say, now curious.

Dean Bariel opens the jewelry box to reveal a pair of

earrings. They're little white rabbits, with purple gems for eyes. That's so cute.

Vega lets out a deep sigh of relief. Just a few more turns.

Malik stands up and walks over to the pile, carefully making his pick. He grabs a small yellow box and carries it back to his seat. Opening it, he reveals a hundred dabloon gift card to a local eatery.

"Vega, it's your turn."

"She's definitely going to take my gift card," Malik says, holding it up to her, but Vega moves past him and right towards Dean Bariel.

"Earrings, please," she says with a smirk.

Dean Bariel hands over the earrings and then looks at Adeib, who is holding fuzzy socks. "Only because I pity the feetless."

It goes on like this for a while, people stealing one another's gifts, until finally it's my turn. I walk up to Vega and gesture for her to hand it over. "Earrings, please," I say, just as she did.

She grins and presents the earrings to me. I take out my hoops and put them in. I'm wearing a tight, purple, crushed velvet dress, and they match perfectly. Doing a little spin, everyone hoots and hollers as I show them off.

"Thank you," I say and lean down to kiss her.

It's already too late when I remember that everyone else is there too.

Alitha shakes her head, smiling.

"Surprise!" Vega says, as if we had the entire thing planned, and we all start laughing.

Dr. Lothial tells us a story of when she played a similar gift exchange game years ago with some friends that resulted in two brothers getting into a fist fight.

Everyone continues eating and laughing, and Aura tells us about the meanings of the songs she picked for tonight's playlist. Dean Bariel gives us another update on the secondary campus, and we all have a jolly good time.

After a while, things start to settle down, and people go home. Most of our coworkers with kids didn't come, and I think about how maybe next year we could do something more family friendly, or have a separate event for families. Vega and Alitha stay behind to help me clean up.

"You really went from having your future-girlfriend as your boss, to your best friend being your boss," Vega says suddenly.

"What can I say, I like who I work with." I giggle.

"Good luck though; I'm sure Alitha is a lot tougher than me."

"I think I'll be okay," I look at Alitha, who smiles.

"I hope next year I have someone to bring," Alitha says, and I realize something... I've never seen her date anyone.

"I'm sure you will," I assure her.

"Just not any from Augury."

Standing in the Illusionary Jungle, we watch Alitha drive away. I go to move, but Vega stops me.

"Nuh-uh. Look up," she says, and I do.

There's a little bunch of greenery with white berries, wrapped in a bright red bow. Mistletoe. Vega grabs me by the hips, pulling me into her warm embrace. She dips down, kissing me fiercely. I'd pity how bad she has to crane her neck to reach me if I didn't know how much she enjoyed our height difference. A pink flush spreads across my cheeks, and I swear I can see some in the green of hers too.

A singular snowflake falls, and I put out my hands to catch it.

"I learned a trick or two from the illusionary mages," she says with a wink.

"Did you get your Christmas wish?"

"Better," I say as Momiji and Freja finally fly down to be with us. "I got you."

INDIGO

Sitting in Vega's lap on my living room floor next to the Christmas tree, we open our gifts. Vega starts with the big box I got her, unwrapping it to reveal a machine that makes both coffee and hot chocolate.

"You love it so much, I figured you could make it at home too," I say, turning to kiss her on the cheek. "Okay, open the other one."

"So bossy," she teases as she reaches for the smaller box. Unwrapping it, she sees the snowglobe. It's from Winter Wonderland's gift shop. "Indigo, it's perfect."

"I think it might make music, but I can't remember. You should check the bottom," I lie.

V flips it over to reveal a golden key. "What's this for?"

"My house, silly."

She presses her forehead to mine, and I close my eyes. This is what love is supposed to feel like.

"Thank you," she says. "Now open the other one I got you."

I grab the box and pause before opening it. "Is this what had you freaking out during Dirty Santa?"

"Fucking yes." She puts her face into her hand, rubbing it. "I neglected to label the two boxes, and I wasn't sure if I had brought the one with earrings or... this one."

Holding up the box, I let out a laugh. "If you lifted it up, you would've realized the weight is totally different."

"Yeah well I'm a dumb ass, so."

"Alright, let's see what had your panties in a twist."

"I do not wear panties."

Unwrapping the box, it's obvious it's a sex toy from the logo. What toy, exactly, is what I'm looking forward to finding out. I open the box, and there's a bright green dildo attached to a black harness... oh my. That's a strap on.

I hold it up to my body and let out a giggle. "I can't wear this, it's way too big."

"It's not for you to wear. It's for me," she murmurs, taking off my tank top. We bought matching pajama sets in a deep green plaid. V strips me of my little shorts before removing her shirt and pants as well.

She picks me up, throwing me onto the couch. "Wanna watch me put it on?"

"Yes please," I say, practically foaming at the mouth.

Vega takes a minute to get herself into the harness, the black straps going around her muscular thighs and overtop her tight fitting boxer briefs.

"Lube?" I ask, and she nods, grabbing a small tube from out of the pocket of her pajama pants. "Oh, so you had this *planned* planned."

"Obviously," she says and licks her lips. She leans a knee onto the couch, while the other leg remains planted to the floor. "Now turn around."

She uses a finger to stimulate my clit while the other

plays with my opening. I can feel myself getting wetter as she toys with my body, sucking on her finger before dipping it back into me. She takes the head of the strap and plays with me, teasing me with the tip.

Vega stands and grabs me by the ankles, dragging me over the arm of the couch until my ass is up into the air. Ever so slowly, she sinks the dildo into me. Her strokes start out long and slow, but gradually she works it deeper into me, picking up the pace of her thrusts.

"V-V-Vega," I stutter, relishing in this pleasure. It isn't the largest toy I've seen, but it's pretty damn big—and she uses it to fill me wall to wall.

She pulls my hair, right at the nape of my neck. "Come here," she says, pulling out of me. Turning me around, she kisses me. It's hot and wet, our tongues clashing as we touch each other with such fervor.

"I want you to fuck me," I say.

"Request approved," she says with a chuckle.

Pulling me up and wrapping me around her body, she holds me as I sink back onto the bright green cock. I moan as she uses her arms to bounce me up and down, kissing me while she does.

Vega finds a rhythm I enjoy and continues bouncing me, thrusting the dildo inside me until I go silent and still for a moment. She kisses me, moaning into my mouth as she watches me come, and I shake and shudder as I reach my release. My muscles continue to spasm as she puts me down, gently kissing me.

V wipes me down with a towel and then covers me in a soft blanket, wrapping me up like a burrito. She pulls me onto the couch, and we snuggle up to one another, rubbing our noses together.

"I love you," I say without planning to. There's no

anxiety as I watch her eyes go wide and wait for her to react, because I know she feels it too.

"You fucking better," she teases, pulling me in for another kiss. "I love you more, little rabbit.

acknowledgments

I have so many people I am thankful for, but I'll try to make this brief. If you're a member of my family, or a close friend of mine that is not a reader, thank you. I am not going to put your name into my horny queer orc romance book, because that feels weird as fuck, but I love you all!

Thank you to my husband, who does not understand my obsession with orcs, or tentacles, but supports me all the same. Thank you for holding me accountable to my goals, and for forcing me not to sell myself short.

A special shout out to everyone who helped me develop this world. It is futuristic and modern, and yet I wanted to pay homage to and stay respectful of the cultures of the very real world we live in today. Thank you to Silvercloud, Lo, Nisha, and Ruthie for answering all my silly questions, and for all your wisdom.

Thank you to my ARC team, Hype/PR team, my reader friends, and author friends for hyping me up and sending me so much love. You made me feel like I could do this. Every comment, every DM, every check in—I will cherish it all forever. You know who you are. Thank you for listening to me.

My creative team... wow I love you guys!

To my friend and formatter Jess, thank you for always helping me, and for all your sisterly advice (even the stuff I don't listen to).

To Amanda, for always being down for an artistic adventure. Thank you for making my chapter headers, map, and logo. I appreciate you!

To Fallnskye Illustration, thank you for illustrating my babies, allowing me to create the cover of my dreams. It's beautiful. I cannot wait to see what you do with the rest of the series. I adore you!

To Abby, my friend and editor, for everything. Thank you for making my story feel appreciated and loved, and for encouraging me to explore this world. I'm so glad I get to work with someone that can send me silly photos immediately followed by capitalization corrections. I wouldn't want it any other way!

Last, but certainly not least, my alphas.

Emilee, you were the first person in the bookish community to accept me and make me feel like I could actually become an author, which is a kindness I can never repay. Thank you for being my friend, easing my endless anxiety, and reading my story. I can't wait for everyone to see the beautiful sapphic romance you'll put out into the world one day!

Rae. What the hell do I even say to you? To my alpha reader, kink authenticity expert, idea-bouncer, and other host of our singular brain cell—thank you. You make me a better writer, a better person, and you have probably listened to an entire audiobook worth of iMessage audios from me rambling about my stories, and you have never complained (to me) once. You and me until the end, bestie.

about the author

Priscilla Rose is a Monster Romance author that currently resides in the hellish swamps of Central Florida with their husband and their cats KitKat and Millie. When Priscilla isn't writing or reading, they spend their time at Renaissance Festivals and Anime Conventions, cosplaying to their heart's content. She is looking forward to showing you her monstrously cute stories, so follow along on her journey...

Printed in Great Britain
by Amazon